DEAR MISSING FRIEND

SUSAN McGUIRK

A STORIED SISTERS SOCIETY NOVEL

Sea Crow Press

Copyright © 2026 by Susan McGuirk
Dear Missing Friend

Published 2026, by Sea Crow Press LLC
www.seacrowpress.com
Barnstable, MA 02630

Paperback ISBN: 978-1-961864-54-2
Epub ISBN: 978-1-961864-55-9
Library of Congress Control Number: 2025950321

Cover design by Black Kat Design

All rights reserved.
No part of this book may be reproduced in any form or by any electronic or mechanical means, including information storage and retrieval systems, without written permission from the author, except for the use of brief quotations in a book review.
This is a work of fiction. All characters, organizations, and events portrayed in this novel are either products of the author's imagination or are used fictitiously.

For Matty

Contents

Prologue	1
Chapter 1	7
Chapter 2	35
Chapter 3	59
Chapter 4	89
Chapter 5	119
Chapter 6	151
Chapter 7	173
Chapter 8	193
Chapter 9	211
Epilogue	221
Author's Note	229
Notes	233
Acknowledgments	249
Book Club Guide	251
About the Author	253
About The Press	255

Inspired by Real People and Events

Not I, not anyone else can travel that road for you
You must travel it for yourself.
It is not far, it is within reach,
Perhaps you have been on it since you were born and did not know,
Perhaps it is everywhere on water and on land.

"Song of Myself," 46
Leaves of Grass
Walt Whitman

DEAR MISSING FRIEND

Prologue

Letter from Catherine

129 Cedar Street
New York City
September 7, 1864

Dear Jane,
He found me. Michael sent a message that landed right in my lap, literally. It came in this morning's newspaper. He placed an advertisement in the Missing Friends notices. Most people probably skip them, but we Irish always read them in the unlikely event we will see someone we know trying to find a lost relative.

After my name leaped off the page, I was so startled that I jumped up and paced around the kitchen. Thinking I must have imagined it, I ran to fetch my seldom-used pair of spectacles, to prove my eyes were not deceiving me. Once they were on, I screwed up my courage to look again. I held the newspaper close to my face. There was no denying what was before me. I copied the notice for you because it may take months for it to be reprinted in the *Sag Harbor Corrector*.

SUSAN MCGUIRK

MISSING FRIENDS

OF Catherine McGUIRK, who when last heard from was in Long Island; she lived in Sack Harbor about twenty years ago. Any information concerning the whereabouts or fate of the above person will be thankfully received by Rev Joseph F Gallagher, Worcester, Wayne county, Ohio.

My heart was thumping so hard I could barely breathe. I ran to my room, as I did not want my employers to be alarmed by the shaking hands of their governess. After I calmed myself, I was still afraid to come out and face them.

I did not tell a soul what I saw. I waited days for a response or an acknowledgment from anyone seeing my name, but none have come. Once the notice gets to your newspaper, my name might be recognized. People in Manhattan only know me as Mrs. Heffernan.

Days have gone by, but I cannot stop reading the advertisement. It took fifteen years since Michael left, but I finally stopped thinking about him. I cannot understand why he would contact me after so long. How strange that he used my maiden name instead of his in the notice. I wonder what including a priest's name means and why he is in the state of Ohio.

Jane, you, of all people, know my aim remains to be free of Michael. It has been more than enough time to be forgotten. My long-sought peace and stability feel threatened, and the last thing I want is a ghost to return to haunt me. When he sailed away the first time, the beginning was almost the end. At this late date, there is no going back. I just want to be left alone. Please advise me, Jane.

Your friend,
Catherine

DEAR MISSING FRIEND

Letter from Michael Heffernan

Pittsburgh Avenue
Wooster, Ohio
February 17, 1871

Dear Cathy,
    At first, we were separate, on either side of a divide. Your head was always in a book, and I was a man of action. You said I was the dreamer, eyes on the horizon, looking for a vessel to board. Yet we both had dreams. My wandering was your rival, but you never stayed in one place long. Your quest was ceaseless, but my journey was waylaid. It was cast aside for the fate we both professed to loathe, while your aspiration was achieved. Our paths overlapped, ran parallel, and then diverged at cross-purposes. You kept your promise, and I broke mine. Like the whales I chased as a young man, you were just out of reach.
    They can sing, you know. I could hear the tunes on their breath a nautical mile away. The specter of their agonizing deaths plagues my dreams. In them, the green hand in the crow's nest bellows the sighting of the blowhole, and the vessel gives chase. The boat is lowered, and the harpooner attacks. The first mate inhales the creature's primal pant while hurling the lance. It fastens. The whale gives a "sleigh ride," dragging the boat violently for hours. The "chimney afire" declares death as torrents of blood spout from the head.
    I wake up shaking with regret for the whales and myself. When a vessel summoned me, I could not refuse. I should have been punished on the seas, the islands of the Pacific, the mines of California, the battlefields of the war, or in the towns of northeast Ohio. Instead, contentment became my burden. It is my penance and why I must wait for redemption.

Your loving husband,
Michael

You will hardly know who I am or what I mean,
But I shall be good health to you nevertheless,
And filter and fibre your blood.
Failing to fetch me at first keep encouraged,
Missing me one place search another,
I stop somewhere waiting for you.

"Song of Myself," 52
Leaves of Grass
Walt Whitman

Chapter One

1841–1845

Letter from Catherine, in Gaelic

Mullinclavin, Ireland
February 14, 1841

Dear Da,
    As the dirt slid off my shovel onto your coffin, Uncle Bryan pressed a parcel into my hand. The cameo pendant of Erca, the first princess of Scotland, lay nestled in the brown paper. My heart stopped to see our family heirloom, handed down to me through generations of ancestor mothers.
    When our family gathered the next day to witness your testament, we now four orphans briefly clasped hands. To my right, the firm grasp of Torlough, our redoubtable "Tor," confirmed his new role as the family patriarch. To my left, Frank's warm bear paw reminded me he was our heart. Young Johnny, only twelve years old, was straggling behind, as usual. You will never read this, yet I know you hear me.

Your loving daughter,
Cath

SUSAN MCGUIRK

Letter from Da, in Gaelic

Mullinclavin, Ireland
February 12, 1841

My dearest children,
　The tales of our ancestors are timeworn, but indulge me in one last recitation. One day, you will bequeath our traditions to your children.
　Our ancient lineage may be as much myth as historical fact. Still, we believe we were descendants of Murtagh MacEirc, the High King of Ireland, in the sixth century. Our troubles began when the English confiscated our land during the Nine Years' War. That act hastened the Tudor Conquest of Ireland in 1605. The purloined parish still bears our name, Termonmaguirk, meaning McGuirk's Sanctuary. It was there we became the "Keepers of the Bell," a relic bequeathed to us from Colmcille, the patron saint of Ireland, along with Saint Patrick. The bell was sworn on to settle disputes and drank from to heal the sick. May it always protect you.
　To escape the scourge of serfdom, you must flee our farm and the stifling lack of a future in Mullinclavin. My dying wish is for your small inheritances to provide you with a better life in America. I ask that Johnny stay behind for a time with your uncle Bryan. As a schoolmaster, he will provide the only chance for him to finish his education. Always remember this vow: "In times of trial, remember the Duty and Honor of the Bell."

Your loving,
Da

༄

Letter from Catherine, in Gaelic

38 Mulberry Street
New York City
July 7, 1841

Dear Johnny,
　This letter is from an Irish boarding house we heard about on the ship. The voyage was long, miserable, and nothing I wish to repeat or

remember. We were surrounded by English people on board who were not friendly. I thought I was brave and ready, but our circumstances already intimidated me.

The term "sea legs" became familiar. When the first foul weather strikes, you become helplessly sick to your stomach, where standing is impossible. The moment the misery becomes unendurable, the winds wane, and you can magically stand again. At that moment, your sea legs have arrived to see you through the rest of the voyage.

No amount of cleaning could remove the nasty stench in steerage. Sleeping next to strangers and lacking proper privacy was a continuing trial that took all my worldly resolve to rise above. The ever-present vermin and monotonous, unsavory food did not help. The chill wind and damp cabin were my constant companions, as was an incessant hacking cough. At least one sympathetic acquaintance on board helped ease the burden. Having a friend to converse with made me forget where I was sometimes.

I am sorry to complain, as we were fortunate to depart of our own will. We are blessed to be young, healthy, and strong, with some money to get us started. I hope I have not discouraged you for your turn.

I am sorry I did not cry when I said goodbye to you. As the *Queen Victoria* pulled away from the slip toward the infinite ocean, my brave facade melted. My yearning for the motherland I would never see again almost strangled me. Missing loved ones and places is new, but it feels indistinguishable from grief. I only hope that the missing return, even if only in our hearts.

Your loving sister,
Cath

Letter from Catherine, in Gaelic

38 Mulberry Street
New York City
October 14, 1841

Dear Susie,

When we met at the townland well to say goodbye, I professed no regrets about leaving. I lied to you, as I desperately miss you and our home. New York is intense and unrelenting. Even Liverpool, where we embarked, is a backwater compared to this human chaos. As jarring as it is, I am strangely drawn to it, as though it were familiar. Of course, that is utterly impossible.

When I saw the skyline of New York City, I felt like Elizabeth Bennett in *Pride and Prejudice*. Perhaps fate had more in store for me than I imagined. At last, I am free of being shackled to a tiny plot of land, watching my life waste away. This is my chance to become a different person, and I do not intend to waste it.

Please, Susie, never let me forget I said this. I declare here and now: "I vow to become a governess in America or die trying." I found a fleeting friend on the ship to whom I also confided my secret ambition. He was the first person I have told besides you and my brothers. Maybe here, a girl can decide for herself what kind of life she wants.

After disembarking, Tor, Frank, and I forged through the teeming crowds to an Irish boarding house on Mulberry Street. Luckily, it is a distance from the riffraff of the Five Points neighborhood, the worst in New York. The idea of gentility can be an antiquated notion here. Women pass us on the street and shout to my brothers, "Come join me, sir." Men openly stare at me, but with two brawny brothers flanking me, they say nothing.

We have been repeatedly warned about gangs of criminals roaming the streets. Sad to say, they are Irish, and we have been admonished to be vigilant to avoid pickpockets. Some gangs, like the Forty Thieves and the Daybreak Boys, do worse than that. However, they say their worst crimes are reserved for each other. Between the rearing horses and the forward people, I feel unsafe on the streets without my brothers.

It has only been a few weeks, but our goal of settling in Manhattan is beginning to seem insurmountable. With all the rejection and nasty insults, it feels like a tall gate surrounds the island, keeping us locked out. The only employment available, a mudlark selling scraps or a ratcatcher, is worse than what we had in Ireland. We were naive, not knowing that the proverbial streets of gold were filled with horse manure and trash. We resolve to keep trying. Wish us luck, dear Susie.

Your oldest friend,
Cath

DEAR MISSING FRIEND

Letter from Patrick Lynch

452 Greenwich Street
New York City
November 29, 1841

Dear Catherine,
 You may be surprised to receive this letter. We did not formally declare our intentions to continue our acquaintance when we parted. However, I better understand now your reasons for spurning my marriage proposal on our last night at sea. The predicted rejection of me by your brothers is one obstacle.
 We have not known each other very long or well. I declared myself to you for fear of never seeing you again. I realize I may not be the prize some young ladies dream of. If you could look beyond my spectacles and slight stoutness, my sincerity is true blue.
 You are different from other young ladies I have met. You have ideas of your own, and perhaps marriage could come between you and pursuing long-held ambitions, as you suggest. This is not a predicament I ever expected. I never had a sister, and I lost my mother at a young age. The ways of ladies are mysterious to me.
 Competing with a young woman's aspirations is not a situation I imagined before. You are the first young lady I have ever met who has declared such plans. However, I have always loved challenges, and your determination intrigues me. Embarking on a new life in a new country is indeed matchless.
 While adjusting to the fact that we will not become husband and wife, I have another proposition. Unless you object, I cannot think why we may not proceed as correspondents. Your company, thoughts, and perceptions have been a pleasure to share. Without the intrusion of your hovering brethren, we might continue our meeting of the minds on paper. Our letters do not have to be kept secret. Still, it would be a relief to speak our minds to one another without interference.
 A single young lady and man corresponding with each other may not be proper. Still, I will forgo propriety for the pleasure of your company on paper if you agree. Sharing our struggles and a sympathetic ear in this godforsaken city may ease our paths forward. If each of us collects the mail at the post office ourselves, keeping our missives private may be possible. Please consider my idea. I am still disappointed that I

will not be taking a beautiful wife. Still, we could both benefit from having a friend in this municipal wilderness.

Your possible penfriend,
Patrick Lynch

~

Letter from Catherine

38 Mulberry Street
New York City
December 20, 1841

Dear Patrick,
    I am sorry that I was compelled to refuse your flattering proposal. Your friendship aboard the *Queen Victoria* was my rock. Our shared walks around the deck in the rain were worth risking my reputation and health. Conversing freely with you meant so much that I looked forward to the frequent squalls. Your kindness and perspective gave me the stamina to tolerate the daily trials of life at sea. If I led you to a wrong conclusion, I apologize. I am unfamiliar with the ways of courtship and did not quite realize we were engaged in one.
    My hesitation is that I have never had a life of my own, and I hope for that chance. My dream is to fulfill my ambition of teaching while I am still young. By refusing your hand, I will probably suffer bitter regret someday. Please understand that you did nothing wrong and much right. Just as I will someday lament refusing your proposal, you will no doubt be relieved one day that I refused you.
    If we correspond, we can learn the outcome of these dilemmas. Therefore, I will be honored to exchange letters with you. Your suggestion of keeping our posts to ourselves is sound. Not that we have anything to hide, but others may misinterpret two adults of different sexes developing a friendship. It is for the same reason that neither of us dares take the hour walk through the muddy streets separating us. It would arouse too many inquiries to visit each other. As you suggested, we both need a friend to rely on in this jungle called New York City.

Your new penfriend,
Catherine

Letter from Patrick

452 Greenwich Street
New York City
January 14, 1842

Dear Catherine,
    I am delighted that we are to be penfriends. This is the only positive event I have encountered since landing on these shores. So far, I am having little luck securing a position. While I have not reached the stage of discouragement, I am skirting the edge. When I return each night, I sit alone in my room, contemplating my reasons for coming here. While I do not question that I made the right decision, I never realized how difficult the challenges would be.
    Perhaps coming here alone is the problem, as my boarding housemates are hard to talk to. When I probe for advice or seek companionship, I am usually disappointed. Although if I had a mate aboard the ship, I might have been distracted from pursuing your friendship. I treasure our correspondence, and it more than makes up for my current state of loneliness. May we have a long and fruitful exchange of letters.

Your penfriend,
Patrick

Letter from Catherine

38 Mulberry Street
New York City
February 27, 1842

Dear Patrick,
    Forgive my slow start to our correspondence, as the long days navigating these streets have left little time. I have some unsettling news. Unfortunately, my brothers and I are admitting defeat and leaving Manhattan. Sadly, this is goodbye, but not farewell.
    After failing to secure employment, the boys heard about labor on a

railroad being built on the eastern end of Long Island. I am not sorry to leave here and will not miss New York City. We can resume our confidential correspondence when I am settled in the village of Greenport, wherever that is.

Your penfriend,
Catherine

Letter from Patrick Lynch

Merchants Hotel
39 Cortland Street
New York City
April 30, 1842

Dear Catherine,

I am sorry we will not be in proximity and for your current travails. It must be daunting to move on again, though I am glad you will not be alone. My solitariness continues to weigh on me, and I am thankful you will continue our exchange.

The good news is my run of bad luck is improving. An acquaintance I encountered from Cork helped me secure a job at the Merchants Hotel as a hall man. I patrol the floors for safety and security, removing intruders who do not belong there. Assisting with the guests' requests is my other responsibility. So far, the labor is tolerable, as the strangers obey me because I am large. The patrons order me about because I have an accent. Please speak up if I am usurping your time from duties and responsibilities with our correspondence. As much as I anticipate it, I do not wish it to become an obligation on your part.

Your penfriend,
Patrick Lynch

DEAR MISSING FRIEND

Letter from Catherine, in Gaelic

Third Street
Greenport, New York
June 19, 1842

Dear Johnny,
　Now that you are in your teen years, I can be frank about our challenges here. Some of them may be your own in time. The boys heard about labor on the railroad in Greenport, a village about a hundred miles east of Manhattan. Leaving the big city was a simple decision. Whatever Greenport was, it had to be an improvement over those horrid streets. With much trepidation, as there was no railroad occupation firmly in hand, we took the chance of boarding another vessel. We hoped it would lead to a new life in a place called the North Fork of Long Island.
　Now that we live in Greenport, whose citizens are descendants of the Puritans, we are tolerated but not much accepted. There is little opportunity for us to socialize or make friends. Many inhabitants work in the whaling industry, which entails long voyages to faraway places. I am grateful our brothers chose local labor, as I would hate to be left alone. Yet they find the railroad trade punishing. The other Irishmen they work with are downtrodden from the back-breaking toil of laying ties.
　I am keeping house in our small rental cottage, trying to keep my spirits up for the boys' sake. The women buying provisions at the market nod but do not respond to my overtures of conversation. We are there shopping for our families, granted from different backgrounds, but it still galls me they consider me alien. I am so removed from a friendly face that I banter with a cat outside our front door. How long I can keep up a stoic demeanor is in question. Perhaps better days are in the offing, dear brother.

Your loving sister
Cath

SUSAN MCGUIRK

Letter from Catherine

Third Street
Greenport, New York
July 18, 1842

Dear Patrick,
    Of course, you are not interfering with any responsibilities I face in this new life. Picking up your letter at the Greenport post office today was a pleasure. It was a balm to my spirits, trampled here too frequently. Cultivating an epistolary friend is a habit I treasure.
    I am pleased that you can show your abilities, and sincerely hope that your position develops into a lasting occupation. Securing professional labor is difficult for any female, but seems especially remote for a foreigner like me in a new village. As I told you at sea, they prepared me to be a teacher at the school I attended. Unfortunately, my dream may be foregone for a long time.
    We have the same challenge of Americans being bothered by our accents, and facing the same obstacle makes me feel less alone. I am trying to learn patience on this side of the sea. I hope your work continues well. When my brothers and I boarded the vessel from New York to begin another new life, my head was bent with fatigue and discouragement, Patrick.
    On this forlorn voyage, I clutched the pendant hanging around my neck with all my strength. The ivory carving is of Princess Erca, the daughter of the first king of northern Scotland and Ireland in the fifth century. I did not care if the pendant's derivation was a fanciful embellishment by an imaginative ancestor. The faded, carved silhouette against the weathered wooden background was still beautiful. It linked me to the princess born, in fact or fable, over a thousand years ago in Scotland. It felt like the last link to everything I had ever known in my eighteen years on earth.

Your penfriend,
Catherine

Letter from Catherine, in Gaelic

Third Street
Greenport, New York
August 30, 1842

Dear Susie,

I am glad that we are far from the crude streets of New York, but we are still struggling. The village of Greenport is not a respite, but another challenge. I fear my brothers will become as browbeaten as the other Irishmen laboring on the railroad. I have urged Tor to implement his original plan of buying a small farm. Frank applied for the shipbuilding trade, but with no other Irishmen in the yard they refused him.

Tor traveled across the Shelter Island Sound off Greenport to Bridgehampton to inspect a property. It is about forty-five miles by land but only ten nautical miles to the nearby port of Sag Harbor. Tor made the journey alone, hoping to send for us if he secured the farm. I would be grateful if you could visit young Johnny for me.

Your oldest friend,
Cath

Letter from Johnny McGuirk, in Gaelic

Kingscourt, Ireland
November 17, 1842

Dear Cath,

I am sorry that adjusting to America is so hard, and I hope things are improving for the three of you. Living and learning with Uncle Bryan and little Jack is better than expected. He is an excellent schoolmaster but exacting of his students. Though I am separated from you and the boys, I still feel like I am in a family.

Without a mam to care for him, Jack is constantly by my side. What a terrible fate to lose your mother in childbirth. I have never had someone who needs me before, and I am no longer the baby of the family. Now, I am a big brother whose help is required to raise one. I do not want to let him or Uncle down.

Your younger brother,
Johnny

⁓

Letter from Catherine, in Gaelic

Tomasina Farm
Scuttle Hole Road
Bridgehampton, New York
April 17, 1843

Dear Susie,
 Frank and I joined Tor on a farm he bought near a village called Bridgehampton. We live in a small house on the land. Tor has christened his purchase Tomasina Farm, which is the combination of our parents' names in Gaelic. When I hear the lilt of the word "Tomasina" spoken aloud, they still seem to be with us.
 The Bridgehampton countryside is picturesque, though so different from Mullinclavin. The soil here is sandy and rocky instead of moist and dark. While Tor is engaged in his new occupation, farming reminds Frank and me of why we left home. The monotony and tedium of plowing, hoeing, feeding chickens, and milking cows are the same.
 While we live with Tor, I help with farm chores. Frank has been walking back and forth to the nearby village of Sag Harbor, searching for labor. It is another whaling port only four miles from the farm, but it seems farther over the pitted, sandy path that serves as a road.

Frank took a temporary room in a hotel in the village to bolster his chances of employment. He promises to send for me when he secures a trade. Though this is another unsettled interlude, our prospects seem promising, considering Tor's successful land purchase. I, too, look forward to finding a home where I belong.

Your oldest friend,
Cath

Letter from Frank

Nassau Hotel
Sag Harbor, New York
July 26, 1843

Dear Cath,
 Sag Harbor is a place of good luck for a lad from Ireland. My English is well understood, especially after all that drilling in grammar our entire childhood. People from all over the world stroll the wharf here. A fellow I talked to about hauling cargo from the vessels told me, "Irish accents are easy compared to those of the people from distant lands who wander the streets."
 Down at the wharf, I noticed something else unusual. There is one place where folks of different sorts seem to get along—aboard these whaling vessels. A hand on the dock told me,
 "We have fellows who are white, free Black, members of the Shinnecock and Montaukett tribes, and from the Azores and Pacific Islands. They all live together in close quarters for years on the voyages." That is remarkable. We were subject to snide remarks and closed doors in the short time we spent in New York City. Maybe our luck is changing, finding our way to this place called Sag Harbor. They will tell me tomorrow whether I have secured labor hauling goods on the wharf. Send me good wishes, Cath, my girl.

Yours forever,
Frank

SUSAN MCGUIRK

Letter from Catherine

Tomasina Farm
Scuttle Hole Road
Bridgehampton, New York
August 14, 1843

Dear Frank,
    Congratulations on joining the trade at the wharf. I am happy for you and know you are making a fine start. Our rightful life in America will truly begin when I join you in the house you rented for us. We tried mightily to save wages to book a passage, unaware of the trials awaiting us. We thought escaping Ireland was challenging, but that was only the beginning.
    All this itinerant wandering since leaving home, from one temporary residence to the next, will finally seem worthy. I strived so much to rise above each situation that it felt like I was constantly floating. It will be a pleasure to finally plant my feet on terra firma. I forget what a true home is like, but our new house will become one, dear brother.

Yours forever,
Cath

Letter from Catherine, in Gaelic

Division Street
Sag Harbor, New York
January 8, 1844

Dear Susie,
    We have settled in our new home in Sag Harbor. It is another whaling port near Tor's farm, and our fortunes are improving. On my first day there, I gaped at the activity, which was a carnival of excitement and novelty. Even as an outsider, I had a perception of the purpose and industry coursing through the village. Everyone had an occupation and was thoroughly engaged in performing their duties.

DEAR MISSING FRIEND

At the wharf, I took in the shops serving the whaling industry: sailmakers, coopers, and those selling riggings and iron goods. Susie, my delight was barely concealed upon finding the lending library. The streets were lined with modern services for such a small village. There is a grocery and liquor store, a general store, taverns, a bakery, a tin shop, a butcher, a jewelry store, a hat shop, a tailor, a shoemaker, a cabinetmaker, a clockmaker, a stationery shop, a drugstore, a blacksmith, a doctor, a post office, and a newspaper office. There is also a Customs House to accommodate Sag Harbor's status as a port of entry for the entire United States.

The narrow sidewalks are perfect for meandering under a canopy of trees that line the small, inviting houses. The din of horses and nasty drivers yelling and cursing, like there was in Manhattan, is forgotten. The lone carriage driver I encountered crossing the street tipped his cap to me. Far from being splattered with mud by the traffic, I emerged from the street without a blemish. My old habit of pressing a handkerchief to my face to ward off the stench was unnecessary. The air smelled sweet and fresh, with a hint of salt from the sea. Unlike in Greenport, the shopkeepers greeted me in a friendly fashion, which warmed my heart. I am already beginning to forget our detour to New York and the neighboring port.

A thoroughfare called Division Street runs down the middle of the village. It casts one side of Sag Harbor in the Town of East Hampton and the other in the Town of Southampton. Frank and I live on the East Hampton side, on the edge of Eastville. It is a community of whalemen, free Black people, and folks from the Shinnecock and Montaukett tribes.

I am encouraged that we are in a neighborhood with a variety of people. It might provide a better chance to fit in. That would mean much after being excluded as foreigners in Greenport and New York City. For the first time since Mullinclavin disappeared from the back of a wagon, we are somewhere we might belong. Susie, you will like this place if you ever come here.

Your oldest friend,
Cath

SUSAN MCGUIRK

Letter from Catherine

Division Street
Sag Harbor, New York
February 11, 1844

Dear Patrick,
Our time in Greenport was a detour, not a destination. From observing my brothers' grueling toil, I admonish you to avoid railroad employment. When Tor purchased a farm nearby, Frank and I moved to a small house in Sag Harbor, another whaling port.
It fills me with joy to have a proper home. I inquired around the village, "Do you know any families who might want to employ a governess?" None of the people I spoke to could name one. It turns out Sag Harbor is made up of tradespeople, not the landed gentry.
My newfangled optimism was still not deterred. I naively believed they would not think me too foreign to at least serve in a role at the local school. The assumption remains that schoolmasters are men, so I did not place my hopes in that position. However, it seemed reasonable that I could become an assistant in some capacity. I told the headmaster, "I achieved a rare Level Five of the Core Five Reading Books back in Ireland." He looked at me as though I was speaking gibberish.
Unfortunately, it seemed no one wanted an Irish immigrant with an accent teaching their American children English literature. Furthermore, the local school did not offer French, which is my favorite subject. It was humiliating to be treated as though I had made an outlandish request when I was more than qualified to teach. I gathered my dignity as best I could despite the nasty sneer on the arrogant face of the headmaster.
After adjusting my expectations, I began knocking on doors around the village, searching for any labor I could find. Following your lead, I secured employment at the Nassau Hotel, admittedly a detour from my lofty ambitions. I assist at the front desk and substitute in the tavern or kitchen when necessary.
Many of the customers come off the whale vessels that arrive regularly. We do not get the riggers and boatsteerers, as they stay at the boarding houses on the wharf. Our patrons are the first mates, officers, and the occasional captain. After a few pints in the tavern, they can still imitate their subordinate brethren. Despite the vagaries of the trade, I am grateful to earn wages for the first time in my life.

My most intriguing customer at the Nassau Hotel has been a former whaleman named Herman Melville. He was a brooding, handsome man with an air of vague menace about him. Mr. Melville confided, "I have just finished a book about my time in the South Pacific, and I am looking for a publisher."

I shook his hand and said, "Congratulations are in order." From the intense look on his face, I presumed some trial had been visited upon him there. Summoning my courage, I asked, "If you do not mind, Mr. Melville, would you describe the South Seas?"

"Tahiti is like a paradise," he said, though his tone made the compliment sound ominous. He became almost transported speaking of it. "The natives' perceptions of time, labor, and love have no equivalent in our way of life. We measure, compete, strive, and classify through the years. They attend, cooperate, defer, and accept whatever happens among them."

I kept nodding, not at all sure what he was talking about. Then he offered me a quote from *Typee*, the title of his book: "However ignorant man may be, he still feels within him his immortal spirit yearning after the unknown future." For this recent immigrant who harbors aspirations beyond my current station, his sentiment spoke volumes.

Mr. Melville told me he had taught school for several years. I confided, "My dearest wish is to teach, but my overtures in the village were soundly rejected."

"Never give up, young lady," he said, which I will not forget. Sag Harbor is undoubtedly a more fascinating place than what we left behind in Ireland. I hope our recent lull in letter writing portends well for your new occupation.

Your penfriend,
Catherine

Letter from Patrick Lynch

Merchants Hotel
39 Cortland Street
New York City
April 19, 1844

Dear Catherine,
    How pleased I am that we are laboring in the same profession. What a fascinating acquaintance you have made in Mr. Melville. Despite my pleasure in our shared occupation, I hope you remember the dream of teaching, as Mr. Melville said.
    The hotel trade is also providing me with fascinating new associates. I met a gentleman named Cornelius Vanderbilt, who frequents the tavern. Some would argue that he is not one, given his crude and aggressive ways.
    Unlike anyone I have ever met, Mr. Vanderbilt fills each room he enters with his bearing. All those present seem to absorb his every word. His hand is in so many businesses that he relies on accountants to calculate his worth. He owns much real estate besides the ferry, steamboat, and railroad companies, all under his purview.
    We have struck up a friendship. He told me, "A bright young man like you might have a place in a venture I will launch soon, especially if you do not mind traveling."
    I assured him, "Mr. Vanderbilt, I would do anything you asked."
    "The next time I am in town, we will speak again," he replied. I am eagerly awaiting his return.
    He lives across the river in New Jersey. While doing business in New York, Mr. Vanderbilt always stays at the hotel. I have tried to study him during each visit and learn from his vast knowledge and business talent. What an honor that he has taken an interest in me, and I will jump at any opportunity to be employed in his firm. Wish me luck upon his return.

Your penfriend,
Patrick

Letter from Catherine

Division Street
Sag Harbor, New York
July 8, 1844

Dear Patrick,
My last letter to you was returned from the hotel with a note on the envelope: "In Panama." I can only assume that you have indeed become employed by Mr. Vanderbilt. Congratulations! How fascinating to be so far away and in such an exotic place. I envy your adventurous opportunity and look forward to hearing about it upon your return.
Perhaps your loneliness will be in the past with this additional responsibility. My work at the hotel continues to occupy me, and I still enjoy living in Sag Harbor. I will patiently wait for your reply whenever you return home.

Your penfriend,
Catherine

Letter from Catherine, in Gaelic

Division Street
Sag Harbor, New York
December 7, 1844

Dear Susie,
How exciting that you and your brother are preparing to emigrate here. To have my best friend with me again will make my homesickness disappear for good. I have never needed a friend to confide in more than now. Susie, please prepare for a big surprise, as I have a new beau. This is how we met.
One afternoon, I struggled up the hotel stairs with some heavy bags. A young man passed, coming down the opposite way. He bent down and slid the bags out of my hands. Susie, I gazed up into the most ravishing blue eyes I have ever seen. He set the bags at the top of the stairs. I was already becoming smitten with this handsome whaleman,

Michael Heffernan. Later, I served him a pint of ale in the tavern. He told me, "I just returned from a two-year-long whaling voyage to the Sandwich Islands and Polynesia."

After the crew unloaded the vessel each day, Michael would stop by the tavern to see me. We talked for hours, about what I could not say. I adored listening to his voice and catching the faraway look in his eyes. After completing the unloading of the vessel, Michael left for Greenport to be reunited with his sister. The minute he was out of my sight, I missed him terribly.

As much as I like Michael, there is something about him I cannot quite fathom. Frank snatched a glance at him on the wharf. He said, "You have a schoolgirl romance based on good looks, not character. Do you know anything about this man?" From Frank's description, Tor said, "He could be a ne'er-do-well."

Michael says little about himself, though solicitous of me. Besides being Irish, I am not sure if we have much in common. We do like to stare into each other's eyes. The chambermaids at the hotel encouraged me to heed the warnings about sailors. They said, "A whaleman will break your heart because they are already married to the sea. They have a girl in every port." Still, as much as the caveats give me pause, I cannot attribute those qualities to Michael. Even though I am almost twenty years old, I have hardly had a caller before, so I need your advice. I will try to wait until you get here before I decide to become Michael's sweetheart.

Your oldest friend,
Cath

Letter from Patrick Lynch

Merchants Hotel
39 Cortland Street
New York City
January 14, 1845

Dear Catherine,

You did indeed guess correctly. I was in Panama and Nicaragua working for Mr. Vanderbilt. I left rather suddenly, and my destinations were so remote that sending letters was unmanageable. We were scouting overland routes through a jungle. Our locations were too far from a port where I could ask a passing ship to take a letter. Regrettably, regarding our continuing correspondence, I am returning to Central America shortly. I am only here long enough for the errands and paperwork required to maintain a residence in New York.

If only you could accompany me on my next trip. I know you have your occupation, but the country's culture and customs would fascinate you. They are so rich and varied that it would take me many letters to describe them.

Let me know if you ever want to change your life in any substantial way. I am always at your disposal to help make that wish a reality. My feelings have not changed, though I understand it would entail your sentiments altering considerably. Of course, we can proceed as usual and let my musings remain in the realm of imagination. I am going to return to Central America soon. Unfortunately, because of the remoteness of the locale, we may experience another rupture in our correspondence.

Your penfriend,
Patrick

Letter from Catherine

Division Street
Sag Harbor, New York
March 11, 1845

Dear Michael,

I have done what you asked and committed the story of my childhood to paper. I hope you will do the same in return, as I long to know more about you.

Our little townland, Mullinclavin, sat near the intersection of four counties. Cavan, Louth, and Meath bordered Monaghan, where we lived, on three sides. I first learned to disbelieve authority at the Irish Society School in Kingscourt, across the county line in Cavan. We were the only family in Mullinclavin to attend there. The state ordered the school to convert us from Catholic to Protestant, which is why few Catholics attended.

The lure my parents could not resist was a superior education in literature, history, French, Latin, mathematics, and science. The subjects were taught in English, not Gaelic, like the local hedge school where my uncle taught. Unlike his school, mine charged no tuition, an added benefit to my beleaguered da.

He trusted that my brothers and I would have the strength to ignore everything the schoolmasters said about religion. My da said, "It will not be easy to question your teachings. Then again, our Irish nature is stubborn, and we doubt authority." Though it took constant vigilance, it was good practice. I also learned to disbelieve the rules I was taught about girls' proper behavior.

Still, being one of the few Catholics in my school was lonely and vexing. The other girls were cruel and teased me, so I played with boys instead. However, believing in the value of an excellent education took no converting at all. I just had to devise a use for it. The occupations reserved for girls—spinning yarn, weaving flax into linen, or sewing lace—were not for me. French was my favorite subject, and I loved to imagine myself in the land of my hero, Joan of Arc.

I suspect that growing up in Mullinclavin was the same road to futility as being raised in Limerick. We toiled on our small farm, growing potatoes and raising livestock. Yet we could never get ahead because of the high rents the absentee English landlord extorted from us. Learning so much about the world in school only made our plight seem worse. Year by year, our lives were shrinking before our eyes. Despite our loving family, nothing could change the inevitable misery the immediate and lasting future held for us.

When our land would be subdivided again for my brothers, there would not be enough to attempt farming. Girls were not a part of the calculation. The so-called prize of making a good marriage was in vain. All the young men faced the same fate as my brothers. Even without Da's parting wish for us to go to America, the only path forward was escape. We reaped one more harvest at Cabra Castle, next to our school, to earn extra wages for the voyage to America. Then we were gone. I look forward to learning about your childhood.

Your sweetheart,
Cathy

Letter from Susie Fee, in Gaelic

Fee Farm
Scuttle Hole Road
Bridgehampton, New York
June 17, 1845

Dear Cath,

I am so happy to have arrived at the farm of my brother Junior in Bridgehampton. I felt ready for the journey from the tale of your passage, which was sadly true. In my lack of bearing here, I did not realize Junior's farm was next to your brother Tor's. "I am so happy to see you!" he greeted me, followed by a hug. It was out of character for your proper big brother.

America seems to agree with the Irish folk here. Seeing family makes me feel at home. I have already visited with some cousins, with more arriving soon.

I will walk over to Sag Harbor the first chance I get. We can have a long talk about your young man. I am so excited that one of us, at least, has a sweetheart.

Your oldest friend,
Susie

Letter from Catherine

Division Street
Sag Harbor, New York
July 22, 1845

Dear Michael,

I was afraid that I would be the only one confiding my life story. Your remote air and distant eyes may have deterred other girls, but they will not deter me. The more you withhold, the more I will ask you about your childhood and what capturing a whale is like. This time, I will not be discouraged by that cloud passing over your face or your downcast eyes. I am still seeking descriptions of the exotic places you have visited, especially Tahiti. Herman Melville raved about it, but you are reluctant to broach the subject.

Events at sea may have marked you beyond your ken. No matter how much I learn about you, Michael, some doors may remain shut. I will keep trying to pry them open so we can become closer, as a couple should be. You are not making it easy, but you are a kind gentleman despite being aloof. I will wait for you to return my gesture and write your history if you dare.

Your sweetheart,
Cathy

Letter from Michael

Fourth Street
Greenport, New York
September 3, 1845

Dear Cathy,

My parents are also gone. I was far away when they passed, something I will always regret. Of course, my mam and da loved me, but the endless grind of having nothing wore them down. Though I dreaded never seeing them again, I was as eager to leave Ireland as you were. I went to a hedge school in Cashel, this one under a roof. By then, the Protestants had deigned to legalize Catholic schools, so we no longer hid behind hedgerows outside to learn. The masters taught us to read and write in Greek and Latin, but not the enemy's language. Once here, with a foundation in the classics, I quickly grasped written English.

My brother William and I landed in New York in 1843. We also found our way to the end of Long Island to labor on the railroad. To escape that drudgery, we became seamen, which separated us. We became the proverbial two ships passing, as we were rarely in port at the same time. It was a lonely life.

My fortunes improved when my younger sister arrived. Her name is Elizabeth, nicknamed Ellen. You are not the only poor girl who has endured living with three brothers her entire childhood. One time, when we were young, the four of us took the wagon to church. Afterward, Ellen was still inside chatting with the neighbors. My brothers and I were hurrying home and forgot about her. Little did we notice her absence until we were hungry. "Where is supper, and why is Ellen not here?" When we went to fetch her, she presided over dinner with our parish priest. "Go home. Get your supper yourselves. I am not ready to leave yet," was her retort to our belated rescue.

Being the only girl in a trio of brothers is not the only thing you two have in common. As Ellen says, "I can run, throw, and wield a hoe with the best of you." We share a house in Greenport, and I will introduce you soon. Now that you have read about my raising, you know I keep my promises. Here is one more. I promise to stay true to you as I embark on my next whaling voyage in a few weeks. Will you promise to wait for me?

Your sweetheart,
Michael

My spirit has pass'd in compassion and determination around the
whole earth.
I have look'd for equals and lovers and found them ready for me in
all lands,
I think some divine rapport has equalized me with them.

"Salut Au Monde!" 13
Leaves of Grass
Walt Whitman

Chapter Two

1845–1847

Letter from Catherine, in Gaelic

Division Street
Sag Harbor, New York
November 15, 1845

Dear Johnny,

    I am not bearing good news, and I hope it does not affect your enthusiasm for emigrating here. Yesterday, a large fire consumed much of the area around our wharf. Many businesses were destroyed, especially those involved with whaling. When we saw the flames in the sky, Frank and I ran over from our side of the village. We arrived just in time to spy the vessel *Thames* consumed by fire. The whale oil that had seeped into the deck caused the flames to roar like thunder and spread to the nearby buildings. We formed lines, passing continuous buckets of water from the sea to the burning structures to douse the flames. We fetched blankets, woolens, and food from our homes to assist those who had lost all their possessions. The fire raged all through the night.

    The next day, the embers were still smoking. People who had never spoken to us approached us to discuss what had happened. Mere acquaintances, whom adversity had converted into neighbors and fellow survivors, hugged us and wept. We spent all day digging, sweeping, and piling up the charred ruins of furniture, goods, and merchandise from the stores.

For one day, we were not citizens divided by race, religion, or nationality, but one community striving together. The whaling captains from their fine houses labored alongside their humbler brethren in the bucket line, hauling water. We were all volunteers trying to save our beloved port.

In the weeks since the fire, I have seen a transformation in our village. So many buildings were damaged or burned to the ground. People brought low and impoverished are rising with renewed energy. They are vowing to rebuild not just what was there before but bigger and better buildings.

This attitude seems a revelation to me. Back home, when despair set in, it lasted for a long time. I wonder if the imperative to hate our English oppressors has made us tired and a bit hopeless. Yet here, in this port, the determination is raw. There has been little fatigue or resignation, just a Yankee energy to fight on. You are going to like America, Johnny.

Maybe this sounds disloyal to you, but for the first time, I believe I could become a citizen of this country. Frank has already vowed to do so. I might have more in common with my Sag Harbor neighbors than I did with the farmers back in Ireland. I also have the energy to fight to better myself. The new Sag Harbor will rise and improve on the last, just in time for you to arrive here. It will remain a place of opportunity. A sturdy pair of hands and a long day's labor will still lead to success.

Frank and I experienced a tragedy in our village, and we will never be strangers here again. We are full participants, not lonely foreigners from far away. It took a fire, but now we are home.

Your loving sister,
Cath

DEAR MISSING FRIEND

Letter from Michael

Faial, Azores Islands
Portugal
December 3, 1845

Dear Cathy,

This voyage is different from any other I have been on. Before, I would listen to my mates share stories, but I rarely joined the conversation. Now I can weigh in when the lads talk about their sweethearts or wives. I show them the daguerreotype of you, my proudest possession. I look at it every night before I sleep and each morning when I open my eyes. Someday I will believe my luck that a lady of refinement, education, and delicacy cares for a deckhand like me. I see you standing against the sea, the wind blowing your golden-brown hair, and it seems like a dream. Happiness is within reach when I doubted it before. You have given me that hope.

I have always been a bit to myself on these voyages despite being surrounded by crew. The captain and his mates sequester in their fine cabins. Montaukett and Shinnecock tribe members are allied, as are the Black harpooner, cook, and steward. The cooper, carpenter, and blacksmith usually think they are above the crewmen. While Joe Josey is my friend, he speaks Portuguese with his brethren from the Azores, and I cannot understand their language. I am usually the only Irishman, and my other solitary mate is from the Pacific Islands. Though we barely understand each other's language, he is good company.

However, our fellowship has limits, as we have different beliefs and have little in common regarding how we were reared. On board, religion takes on more of the flavor of our Shinnecock and Montaukett crew members. They see the Almighty in the wind and the storms, and after time away from churchgoing, we all follow suit. There is no sabbath or day of rest at sea. Those back home may find that blasphemous, but I prefer it to how superstitious most of the crew are. Unfortunately, that may also be because of the inherent danger in this occupation. They see the deaths and accidents at sea and try to ward off becoming an ill-starred voyage. They do not realize that their silly habits and repetitions will not protect them.

The monotony of day after day at sea troubles me less with you to engage my thoughts. There is a sense of peace going through the days, knowing you are missing me. Even during foul weather, I am less unsettled than before. Your brothers object to me, but eventually, they will relent when they see how much we love each other. I will prove that I am worthy of you, just as any man courting my sister would do. I am enjoying this brief time in Faial, Azores Islands, as I accompanied Joe Josey to visit his family here. They are fine people who helped me plan a surprise for you, but I will not spoil it.

From here, we sail to the Cape Verde Islands off the coast of Africa to take on more food and supplies. It may be weeks before we disembark again as we head to Cape Horn, at the tip of South America. After we sail around it, we enter the Pacific Ocean. Once there, we will spend some time in the Sandwich Islands, where I can post a letter to you again.

Your sweetheart,
Michael

Letter from Catherine

Division Street
Sag Harbor, New York
January 28, 1846

Dear Michael,

I hope this letter will reach you by the time you make landfall in Hawaii. More patience is required on my part to stop missing you. I have met no one like you before. Until the recent past, the only men I have known were farmers. You could not be more different and could even be considered opposites. While farmers are predictable, sailors are mysterious. One never knows where they will appear next. Farmers stay in one place and can always be found. They know a great deal about the confines of their land, but little beyond.

Men of the sea have no lack of adventure as their vessels sail to the next port. They like movement and gazing upon vast expanses. Farmers plow up and down their rows with their heads down. Sailors have seen exotic lands and strange practices about which the rest of us know nothing. Please tell me more about them because they are unimaginable in my limited experience. If I were a man and had to choose, I would be a sailor rather than a farmer. Better still, I would stay true to my instincts and become a governess.

Perhaps you started the book I gave you, *The Pathfinder*, by Frank's favorite author, James Fenimore Cooper. I picked it because Cooper also lived in Sag Harbor and worked in the whaling business about twenty years ago. I am on tenterhooks, waiting to see what my surprise is. Please take care of yourself, Michael.

Your sweetheart,
Cathy

Letter from Michael

Honolulu, Hawaii
Sandwich Islands
March 21, 1846

Dear Cathy,

How happy I am to receive your letter. I remember the first night we talked in the tavern after I met you on the stairs. Though I was afraid to say it then, you were the most beautiful girl I had ever seen, not to mention the most intelligent and accomplished. That you are my sweetheart still astonishes me.

The voyage is on course, though we have not caught many whales. Rounding Cape Horn, we sailed north along the coast of South America, making a stop at the Galapagos Islands. The giant tortoises are a wonder to behold. I am relieved to be in Hawaii eating fresh food after surviving on hardtack, pork, and salt horse for weeks. The captain was so angry with our failure to capture whales that he threatened to sail to the Arctic. However, he makes an empty threat, as no whale vessel has ever traveled that far north.

We fastened a whale several times when the fog rolled in, or the weather turned rough. Unfortunately, we had to cut the lines, which was demoralizing with so few sightings. When we are at a disadvantage in visibility or movement, better for the whale to sink than our vessel. Equally frustrating is watching a whale swim away when the foul weather renders us unable to lower the boats.

We also suffered a setback when one of our officers became ill. The captain ministered to him, but nothing in his medicine bag worked. He wasted away each day until he expired. We gave him a burial at sea. It entailed wrapping his corpse in canvas and sewing a brick near his feet. On deck, the captain performed the service. He concluded with the words, "We now commit this body to the deep." It chilled me to hear. The body was pushed down the gangplank into the sea. All that was left of the officer were some bubbles from below the surface.

I do not want to frighten you unduly, but by now, you have heard stories around Sag Harbor. I would not be forthcoming if I did not mention that we lost a green hand when he fell from the crow's nest. He was still in his teen years, and it made me cry like a baby. Whenever it happens, we record the poor victim as being "lost at sea." The same was done for the officer who died of illness.

Between the deaths, lack of whales, and accounting troubles, our failures mean we will sail home sooner than expected. Usually, I would be very disappointed with the prospect of my lay being reduced, but not this time. Our unexpected detour is a blessing, even if unlucrative, as I am eager to get home to you.

I started the book you gave me, *The Pathfinder*. Regrettably, I am not much of a reader, especially in English. I will pursue it more diligently and report to you next time. A book is a helpful diversion on deck during the long days at sea. I am not adept at scrimshaw like some of the crew. Mostly, I treasure the book as a gift from you.

I wrote to my sister in Greenport about you, and she wants to meet you when I return. Our brother William was there with her but recently went to sea, so she is alone. Luckily, she has friends at the hotel where she works. I hope our vessel will be sailing homeward toward you by the time I next write.

Your sweetheart,
Michael

Letter from Catherine

Division Street
Sag Harbor, New York
May 23, 1846

Dear Michael,

I pray your vessel is sailing home. I want to be your dearest, but my brothers have compelled me to reconsider becoming a seaman's sweetheart. Still they cannot change how much I care for you. They have the usual warnings of absence and loneliness. Those are of grave concern to me, but they are not my greatest fears.

I am having doubts because I am concerned more about your safety than the pain of our separation. Now that I know more about whaling, I see how many local men have been lost at sea. At first, I was not aware that the rate of mortality was so high. I am not the sort of woman who can take that in stride. The local ladies can better cope, but I am not of their ilk. I am a creature of the soil, not the sea.

I am fearful that we are too different. To ask you to be untrue to yourself is unfair, and I have already failed at the same task. Making these points during your voyage may be harsh, but there was no chance before you left. If I wait until your return, I am afraid I will lose my nerve to address them.

Despite our differences, I can speak my mind with you. Unlike most men I have met, you do not assign me the typical role acceptable for young ladies. The reason I care for you is that you accept my faults. I can express myself freely without fear of being demeaned or told to be quiet. I appreciate that you are not condescending, but it does not prevent my continuing concern for your well-being. Hurry home, my darling.

Your sweetheart,
Cathy

SUSAN MCGUIRK

Letter from Michael

Cape Verde Islands
July 9, 1846

Dear Cathy,
    Please give me a chance and reconsider your brothers' warnings. My only concern in this world is being with you. Whaling does not come close to you in my esteem. To convince your brothers to accept me, I will do whatever is required. If it means forsaking my chosen profession of seafaring, then so be it. Please wait for me, and we will solve the problem together. We will not be apart, I promise.
    You said I do not confide in you enough, and we still need to become better acquainted. I remember how we both enjoyed taking long walks together. We would stroll for hours around the village, basking in each other's company.
    I foresee a long and happy life together for us. Someday we will raise our children until we are old. We will walk the streets of Sag Harbor in our dotage. Each of us will hold up the other so our tired legs will not fold beneath us. That would be a very fortunate outcome indeed. Even when you are a grandmother, you will still be beautiful in my eyes.
    Until I am back to defend myself, I hope you can resist your brothers' exhortations against me. Please do not lose faith in me, mainly because the vessel is pointed homeward. It will not be very long, my darling. Please wait for me.

Your sweetheart,
Michael

Letter from Susie, in Gaelic

Fee Farm
Scuttle Hole Road
Bridgehampton, New York
August 14, 1846

Dear Cath,
    You seem more of a grown-up lady now that you have a sweetheart.

Soon you will be too important for the likes of me. It might be nothing, but your brother Tor acts strangely around me. When we meet, he becomes tongue-tied and drops things, which is so unlike him. You can tell him for me, "Susie is safe and will not bite you." My brother claims, "Tor is sweet on you." As his only sister, I hope you can find out the truth. How lovely it would be if we each had a beau at the same time.

I love being here, but my older brother thinks he is my father since Da stayed in Ireland. My big sister, Ann, thinks she is my mam even though my real one is on the way. Only my younger brother, Charles, acts as before, probably because we are only a year apart. He follows in Michael's footsteps, saying he will sign on to a whaling voyage. My sister and brother are quite upset but cannot convince Charles otherwise. He should be on his way before Mam comes, or there will be a battle when she hears. I will come to visit soon.

Your oldest friend,
Susie

Letter from Johnny, in Gaelic

Kingscourt, Ireland
October 3, 1846

Dear Cath,

The famine is raging. Monaghan is one of the better counties, but it still frightens and upsets me. The west and south are at the gates of hell. The flax is still spun into linen, and the lace is sewn here, though not like before. At least we do not have people starving in the streets like in Counties Clare and Mayo.

Uncle Bryan continues with his school despite the setbacks, and I am progressing in my studies. Thank you for the latest contribution to my passage fund. I aim to come next year, but planning has become folly in these famine times. However, I am managing fine for now with our uncle. I am eager to help with Jack to repay him in kind. I would hate to leave them in a time of need.

Your younger brother,
Johnny

Letter from Catherine

Division Street
Sag Harbor, New York
November 4, 1846

Dear Patrick,
 Once again, the hotel returned my letter with the words "In Nicaragua" on the envelope. So much has happened over an extended period that I do not know where to begin. The same must be true for you. It is challenging to start at the beginning and try to cover so much information. It may be advisable to wait until you return to the United States. I do not want to risk another returned envelope when I have so much to tell you.
 Believe me, your kind words are appreciated. At some point, we will continue our regular correspondence again, I sincerely hope.

Your penfriend,
Catherine

Letter from Susie, in Gaelic

Fee Farm
Scuttle Hole Road
Bridgehampton, New York
December 14, 1846

Dear Cath,
 My brother left on his whaling voyage. Our mam is angry, but it does no good. He said, "I hear the call of the sea," but I do not believe that for a moment. Being a seaman was something Charles Fee had never heard or thought about. How someone who grew up with his hands in the soil can say, "I need salt air," is vexing. I am sure he used that Irish silver tongue of his to talk his way on board. Not having any savings to buy a plot of land like our older brothers may have hastened his choice.

At least he is young and has not left a wife or sweetheart behind. Do not let anyone tell you that Michael's example made Charles leave. He got the idea from the Squires boys next door. Both brothers helped convince Charles to go to sea and join the Presbyterian Church. Charles now has my mam attending there, even though she converted to Catholicism long ago when she married. How quickly heads can be turned here. If only Da were well enough to come, he would stop this. Mam says she plans to return to Ireland to join him, but I do not believe her.

With seventy ships filling the harbor, no wonder they are looking for sailors. Just because it pays better than farming does not mean it is safe. That is how they trick green hands like my relatives. I am told one or two sailors are lost on many voyages. Thank goodness Michael's vessel is headed homeward. In a short time, my young cousins will also leave. Oh Cath, Mullinclavin seems like a lost dream, and the memory fades more each day.

Your oldest friend,
Susie

Letter from Catherine, in Gaelic

Division Street
Sag Harbor, New York
January 9, 1847

Dear Susie,

If only we could be closer. I need a day at liberty from my position to see you, as it takes hours to walk four miles round trip with my feet sinking into the sandy soil. It makes it seem like you are farther away than you really are. I can get lonely during the week with just Frank to talk to and Michael at sea. Lately, I have struck up a friendship with Jane Perdue, a woman who works for the family next door. She differs from anyone in Ireland, as she is a member of the Montaukett tribe and descended from free Black whalers.

We must pick our times to chat. Jane's employer, Mr. Mulford, had family who owned slaves before they became illegal in New York in 1827. Almost twenty years later, Mr. Mulford still regards Jane as though the law has not changed. I quickly knew better than to walk into their yard or call out a greeting to Jane. It was worth being careful so that he would not cast his condescending and withering gaze on me. Mr. Mulford could make Jane's life a misery if she displeased him for any reason. I usually wait until I see Jane at the shops to confide in her and enjoy her company.

Your oldest friend,
Cath

༄

Letter from Jane Perdue, under the front door

Division Street
Sag Harbor, New York
February 7, 1847

Dear Catherine,

I saw you pining for your young man. I was not free to speak with you because Mr. Mulford had his eye on me. You have told me you want to be a teacher. First, I must ask you to be my student because there is a lesson to learn. This time I will not wait until we are at the shops to tell you. I will write down my lesson so you can share it with your brothers, who could also learn.

Your family does not know the story of our village. Our local folk respect the one thing that provides for us all, the whale fishery. Michael's employment is part of our pride and purpose. My people have been whaling for hundreds of years. Our spiritual traditions honor our sacred bond with whaling and the whales themselves. All beached or caught whales are offered in thanks to the spirit Moshup, the giant who sent them to us.

The Montaukett people lived here for many generations before the colonists came and took our land. The only territory they left us is Indian Fields, a small settlement in Montauk. My father left there because there was no labor, and it was too far from the other South Fork villages. I am also from a family of free Black whalers on my mother's side. People of both groups come together down the street at Saint David African Methodist Episcopal Zion Church in Eastville. Tell your brothers that whaling is fine labor for any man. They should stop fretting over the employment of your young man.

Your friend,
Jane

Letter from Catherine, left in the shed

Division Street
Sag Harbor, New York
February 9, 1847

Dear Jane,
Knowing the possibility of a deeper meaning to Michael's chosen profession comforts me, especially when I fear for his safety. What keeps me up at night is knowing few occupations are as dangerous as hunting whales on the high seas. With Michael on the other side of the world, any deity watching over him is welcome news.

Learning of the persecution of your people by the English has resonated with me. The English stole our land, too, though the treatment your forebears endured is far more brutal and enduring. Your lessons occupy my thoughts as I spend the days laboring at the hotel. Your struggles make my paltry concerns seem small indeed. Still, as much as I hate to admit it, my longing for Michael weighs me down. That we are neighbors feels fated.

Your friend,
Catherine

SUSAN MCGUIRK

Letter from Jane, under the door

Division Street
Sag Harbor, New York
February 11, 1847

Dear Catherine,
   It may be a while before I can meet at the shops, so I will write this down. I saw you moping about again this afternoon over that sweetheart of yours. You are no different from the women of Sag Harbor of any color who miss their men at sea. My husband, Silas, has been gone on voyages most years. Almost all the men I know and grew up with here are also whalemen. Like the rest of us, you must learn the ways of a whaling widow. That is what we call the women left behind while their men are at sea.
   First, stop pitying yourself. You have a house to keep and labor to do, and there is no time for whining. Women must look out for themselves. I do not just mean day-to-day. You need to save some wages you earn. I am saving mine to buy a house, and keep them hidden in a box no one can find. I will take you up to one of the widows' walks on the roof of a neighbor's house. You can search in the distance for vessels on the horizon. No one knows why, but it helps us widows settle our souls. I will bring you to the A.M.E. Church, where the spirit of brotherhood will lift you.
   Cooking and cleaning for the Mulford family is one thing the spirits sent me here to do with my life. They have taught me that what I see before me is not all there is. What is not seen is just as important. I must trust and wait for things to turn out right. My body is mine, and while it can be lent to others, they cannot own it. I believe there is more ahead for me, and for you too, Catherine.

Your friend,
Jane

Letter from Catherine, left in the shed

Division Street
Sag Harbor, New York
March 12, 1847

Dear Jane,

Please forgive my wallowing. You are right about what you said. "What a blessing that you have a good position, Catherine, one that would not be available to me." I see every day the trials that are visited upon you that do not apply to me. Your example of strength inspires me daily. Thank you for being patient enough to teach a "thick Irish" student like me. With all your responsibilities, it shows enormous generosity and caring.

I have demonstrated more than once that I have a problem seeing beyond the nose on my face. Why you have patience with me is a mystery, but I am grateful. I baked you a pie with the apples from our tree. Hopefully, it will convince you that I sometimes think of others besides myself.

Your friend,
Catherine

Letter from Catherine

Division Street
Sag Harbor, New York
March 13, 1847

Dear Patrick,

This is a difficult letter to write. I am hoping, by now, that you have returned to New York. We have long since made peace with our standing as friends. I sincerely hope my news does not threaten it. I have met a young man, and we are serious about one another. He will return from a whaling voyage soon, and a proposal is probably imminent. I am sorry if this is hurtful news. While I cherish and depend upon your friendship, I would not want to cause a rift between us.

I hope your association with Mr. Vanderbilt continues, as it sounds most promising and exciting. I look forward to breathing a sigh of relief that my news has had no negative bearing on our friendship.

Your penfriend,
Catherine

Letter from Tor

Tomasina Farm
Scuttle Hole Road
Bridgehampton, New York
June 5, 1847

Dear Cath,

My acres are accumulating, and so far, I have planted crops of potatoes, barley, and buckwheat for the fall harvest. However, my purpose in writing is not farming news. Before his voyage ends, this is the ideal time to warn you against becoming Michael Heffernan's wife. By now, we are acquainted with the local whaling life. As far as I can discern, there is no place within it for a wife and mother. The last thing I want or imagine for you is the title "Whaling Widow." You deserve much more, and I cannot stand silently by and disregard your choice.

Some whalemen are decent fellows, but any man who hates farming as much as Michael is suspect in my eyes. Yes, he is from similar circumstances as our own. Still, I cannot discount the realization that the name Heffernan in Gaelic means demon from hell. I am not superstitious, though the legend of Saint Patrick driving the devil down occurs in Cashel, his hometown.

When Michael came by the farm with you before he left, he was too quiet and not forthcoming. I could not tell what he was thinking, which may portend untrustworthiness. A stable man is of the earth, not the sea. I cannot sit idly by while my sister puts herself in a position to be abandoned. These are signs you should consider one of the other fine young Irishmen who have come to our region. Frank agrees with me, and I have urged him to weigh in. There is still time.

Your brother,
Tor

Letter from Frank, left on the bureau

Division Street
Sag Harbor, New York
July 17, 1847

Dear Cath,

I am committing this message to paper at the behest of our older brother. He thinks you will take the warnings more seriously this way. Also, I retreat as soon as I see your little foot stamping. While I am not as adamant on the subject as Tor, I also have misgivings about Michael as your potential husband. Yet, even as I write this at Tor's request, I am not fit to reproach you by his estimation.

Our brother has declared my newfound infatuation with an Irish newcomer as a greater example of being blinded by beauty than yours. Her name is Isabella O'Brien, and I met her at church. It is true that she is lovely to behold, but we have not come close to actual courting. Tor jokingly suggested we arrange a Sunday visit for Isabella and Michael to become more acquainted. I am sure you agree it is not humorous. He should have been more understanding, as he began courting Susie Fee as soon as she arrived.

However, that does not change my wariness about your choice. Isabella and Susie are not planning any departures, but your sweetheart could disappear at any moment. Cath, my girl, I would hate watching you suffer when this tableau inevitably unfolds. Other than his profession, I do not dislike your suitor. I just do not believe for a minute that a seaman will forsake the sea. Please ponder this deeply, my girl, as the choice is for the whole of your life.

Yours forever,
Frank

SUSAN MCGUIRK

Letter from Susie, in Gaelic

Fee Farm
Scuttle Hole Road
Bridgehampton, New York
August 3, 1847

Dear Cath,
    It looks like your help is not needed, as your brother has made his intentions toward me plain. Like you, I have hardly been courted, which makes it more exciting. Also like you, my big brother is ordering me to go slowly and take my time. Unlike your courtship, there is no story about how we met. Girls usually like to confide such things to a friend, but I have known Tor every day of my entire life.
    Hearing stories about a brother as a beau is not as pleasing as hearing about a daring seaman like Michael. After all, you have known your brother forever, too. Instead, I will try gossiping with my sister, Ann. Then again, she will find fault with me, as she usually does. Just as Michael is sailing home, my brother Charles will pass him. He will be sailing in the other direction out to sea. I will see you soon to ask you for more advice on how to be a sweetheart.

Your oldest friend,
Susie

༄

Letter from Michael

Fourth Street
Greenport, New York
August 25, 1847

Dear Cathy,
    We made land in Greenport, so I will come to Sag Harbor after I collect my lay. I plan to get down on one knee and propose the traditional way. I have so much to tell you and need to gather my thoughts. To be worthy of you in your brothers' eyes, I have decided to quit the whaling trade. This has been a tough decision for me and one I do not

take lightly. I will surely miss the adventure, the camaraderie, and the wind in my face on an open sea.

Cathy, you mean more to me than all of that. I want to be the husband you deserve and hope you will agree to be my wife. Your example is hard to live up to, and I fear disappointing you. I can only try to do my best. Perhaps it will never be enough for your older brother, but I will not stop trying to change his mind. What employment I will pursue now remains a mystery, but I hope to secure something to make you proud.

Instead of the traditional Irish Claddagh version, I bought you an engagement ring with a stone made of chrysoberyl. It is a precious mineral of a pale golden hue found in Portugal. Our first stop of the voyage was in the Azores Islands. There, I purchased the ring with the help of my shipmate and friend, Joe Josey. He explained that chrysoberyl helps you see both sides of a situation or problem. The Portuguese believe it fosters compassion and generosity and promotes forgiveness. For over a year, I have kept the ring safe in my pocket on a seafaring vessel navigating the world. Soon, I will be there to place it on your finger and ask you to be my wife. Please say yes, my love.

Your sweetheart,
Michael

Letter from Catherine

Division Street
Sag Harbor, New York
September 19, 1847

Dear Johnny,

On September 18, 1847, at Saint Andrew's Church in Sag Harbor, Tor reluctantly gave me away, and I became Mrs. Michael Heffernan. It was a simple wedding, and I wore a white dress, though not in honor of Queen Victoria. I chose not to follow her fashion of carrying flowers so no one would think an English queen influenced me. After the ceremony, we celebrated with a cake I baked.

Our brothers will not believe that Michael has finished with the sea. They predict I will be left alone, like another whaling widow. Tor did not hide his displeasure from the groom, while at least Frank feigned cordiality. I missed you that day and cannot wait for you to come.

Your loving sister,
Cath

⁓

Letter from Catherine

Division Street
Sag Harbor, New York
September 25, 1847

Dear Patrick,

    I assume you have not returned, as I have not heard from you. It has been a busy, eventful time, culminating in my marriage to Michael Heffernan. He is the now-former whaleman I told you about. Having just arrived from a long voyage, he and I became caught up in a whirlwind engagement and marriage.

    We have not corresponded lately, and I hope this news will not come between us. Forgive me if I am being cavalier toward your feelings in offering the following disclosure. As I trust you implicitly, you are the only person I have the nerve to admit the following to. On the happiest day of my life, I held Tor's arm, walking down the church aisle. My mam's voice was whispering in my ear. Clutching the pendant of Princess Erca that she bequeathed to me, I heard, "Remember, dearie, never make the mistake of marrying a dreamer." I told myself, *That was just bridal nerves.*

    As I let go of my brother's arm, I strode forth alone to take Michael's hand at the altar. The following week, he secured employment in the shipyard over in Greenport, and once more, I began…I mean, we… began again. Wish me luck, Patrick.

Your penfriend,
Catherine

⁓

Letter from Patrick

Merchants Hotel
39 Cortland Street
New York City
October 29, 1847

Dear Catherine,

Your letters awaited me upon my return from Central America. Have no fear, dear friend. I will not abandon our friendship. Then again, do not expect me to shout hooray from the rooftops. Still, I wish you much future happiness. I am glad you found someone to share your life with and that you will never be alone. Please do not fret about me. While I continue as a solitary man, at least my time is filled with exciting prospects. Congratulations and best wishes on the celebration of your marriage.

Not that there is no envy of your husband, as ungallant of me as that is. As crestfallen as I am, I learned to live with disappointment a long time ago in Ireland. I can certainly accept it as a grown man. One could say I made it my specialty. I try to preserve what I can obtain instead of yearning for what is out of reach. That is why a friendship with you is so precious to me. I will always cherish it, even if it was not my original intention.

I am busy preparing for yet another voyage. My address in New York will continue to be the Merchant Hotel. I have long since graduated from the staff quarters to a fine room with a view. Mr. Vanderbilt wants me to accompany him to Nicaragua again. This time, we will establish a new company that I will be managing. I believe fortune has smiled upon me, as this may be a considerable opportunity. I will report back when I am next in New York. Once again, congratulations.

Your penfriend,
Patrick

Has anyone supposed it lucky to be born?
I hasten to inform him or her it is just as lucky to die, and I know
it.
I pass death with the dying and birth with the new-wash'd babe,
and am not contain'd between my hat and boots,
And peruse manifold objects, no two alike and every one good,
The earth good and the stars good, and their adjuncts all good.

"Song of Myself," 7
Leaves of Grass
Walt Whitman

Chapter Three
1847–1849

Letter from Johnny, in Gaelic

Kingscourt, Ireland
November 20, 1847

Dear Cath,

Congratulations on your marriage. I look forward to meeting my new brother-in-law when I come. Please do not take much of our brothers' words to heart because you know better. The effects of the famine continue to be frightful but endurable for us, at least this far east. Many farmers have left or died, and so much land is untended. The nearby Carrickmacross Workhouse contains many paupers. It is a dismal place where hopeless people who have nothing left go to die.

My escape is my studies. If I could not immerse myself in them, I would be miserable. Thank you for your contributions to my passage, and I will come soon. The three of you have become impatient with me, and I apologize. Uncle Bryan has urged me to get on my way and does not expect further help. However, after all that he has done for me, I still want to contribute my support. It will be sooner rather than later, I promise.

Your younger brother,
Johnny

SUSAN MCGUIRK

Letter from Susie, in Gaelic

Tomasina Farm
Scuttle Hole Road
Bridgehampton, New York
November 28, 1847

Dear Cath,
   Now that the excitement from our respective marriages has died down, it is wonderful to be a newlywed wife. I spend my time between housekeeping and outdoor chores, but farm life is different here than in Mullinclavin. I just closed the icehouse out back used for storing fresh food. Now, we switch to storing food in the cellar for the winter. Last year, Tor kept vegetables, cider, pork, beans, buckwheat, and potatoes from the harvest down there. The barn is full of corn, rye, hay, and wheat. Soon I will take the grain to the grist mill in Watermill to be ground into flour. I thought I might be lonely here, but a steady stream of peddlers visits. The knife grinder was just here, and a cobbler came by asking to repair shoes.
   Despite the ill will about your marriage, I wish you and Michael a lifetime of health and happiness. I look forward to many happy years raising our families together. Our children will be best friends, just as you and I are. You will always be the girl I ran down the hill with. We ran from Mullinclavin to Kingscourt, letting the wind blow us along.
   I always wished I could be brave like you, Cath. You could keep up with any of your brothers when mine laughed at me. Please do not fret that Tor hates Michael. He does not have faith in many people, including Frank, no matter how much he loves him. He will change in time. I know you remember that sometimes Tor can be quite sweet when he wants to be. He is teaching me to write English, and I will start mixing in words as I progress.

Your oldest friend,
Susie

Letter from Catherine

Fourth Street
Greenport, New York
November 30, 1847

Dear Frank,

It seems like another world returning to trying memories in Greenport. The village has grown in the three years since we were here. Life still revolves around the wharf and the whaleships coming and going. The shops are still fewer and less varied than in Sag Harbor, but at least there are more than before. More foreign visitors and immigrants are here now, so we attract less attention for being different.

This time, I am more careful looking for an occupation, as Greenport's insularity is still evident. When I inquire about employment, I knock on the doors around the village, and people pretend they do not understand my accent. They ask me if I am a follower of the Pope and worse. I prefer a woman to answer the door, as I dread any insinuating remarks when men inspect my references.

Michael knows nothing of my daily travails, and I try not to let on how many doors shut abruptly. He is having enough trouble adjusting to shipbuilding. I already miss the bustle and tumult of all the different kinds of people walking the streets in Sag Harbor. Here, everyone appears to be related to each other in a closed club. We foreigners are not members and probably never will be. Thanks for listening to me complain about your former home, dear brother.

Yours forever,
Cath

SUSAN MCGUIRK

Letter from Frank

Division Street
Sag Harbor, New York
December 10, 1847

Dear Cath,

   Aye, Cath, my girl, you sound a bit discouraged. Please do not be, as all will be well. Among much else, we survived Greenport once, and I have no doubt you can again. I know I have been critical about you marrying Michael. I promise: Henceforth, I resolve to be more bountiful and charitable in my estimation of your husband. Michael is trying to become a landlubber. We have not seen many men effectively turn their backs on the whale fishery, and I salute him for trying.
   Michael decided to change his occupation for you, which shows strength of will and character. I give him credit and wish him success, especially for your sake. That you will not be left alone without his wages for three years, like so many neighbors, is reassuring. Though you must adjust to Greenport again, I am encouraged that you are in a happy, stable marriage.
   My courtship is a strange one. Isabella is another only girl in a group of brothers. They came from County Mayo, and the family had a terrible time during the famine. So far, my only meetings with her have been at church with the four burly O'Brien kinsmen surrounding her. I had to address her through a forest of suspicious glares and grunts. It was worth the effort to observe her bewitching smile.
   Labor at the wharf keeps me occupied. Still, I sorely miss my companion down the hall. It is not just because the house is no longer tidy. Your laugh, Cath, my girl, revisits me. I often turn and look behind me, thinking I hear it. If I ever penetrate the wall of cattle encircling a particular young lady, maybe I will not be as lonely.

Yours forever,
Frank

Letter from Catherine, in Gaelic

Fourth Street
Greenport, New York
December 15, 1847

Dear Susie,

I have finally found employment at the Wyandanch Hotel. Michael's sister Ellen, who works there, helped me. They also accommodate whalemen like my previous employer, but they are easier to serve, knowing Michael is no longer among them. While the patrons can be less than genteel, the proprietors are kind and treat me respectfully. Jane told me, "The hotel was named for our sachem, or chief, of the Montaukett people in the mid-1600s, Wyandanch."

At least there are more visitors to the village in the various hotels and boarding houses compared to years earlier. Michael's sister Ellen, who lives in the Wyandanch staff quarters as a chambermaid, has made our move less lonely. Having a woman near my age with whom I can begin a friendship is lovely. Maybe she is a bit boisterous because she is the lone girl with her brothers. Her cackle of a laugh and teasing remarks echo through the hotel halls. Mam would have corrected me for the same behavior, brothers or not. Like her fellow chambermaids, Ellen looks for prospective husbands among the whalemen in the tavern. Thus far, she has had no luck.

Married life is all I could hope for, but Michael's restlessness reminds me of my dissatisfaction with farming. When I ask him about it, he jokes and says, "Are you trying to get rid of me? Maybe you have another sweetheart." I wonder if he is even suited for shipbuilding, as it occupies less of his time. Labor there is reduced due to the dwindling prospects of the whaling business. Sometimes, he seems as impossible to catch as a falling star, yet he stands right before me. I am swept up in his whirl, holding on, hoping not to be flung to the ground. Still, our abiding love keeps my nagging doubts and worries at bay. Thanks for listening, dear Susie.

Your oldest friend,
Cath

SUSAN MCGUIRK

Letter from Catherine

Fourth Street
Greenport, New York
December 18, 1847

Dear Jane,
    As you advised, I have saved some of my wages for the future. To avoid any explanations, I use the wedding hope chest inherited from my mam as a convenient hiding place. I found Michael wandering along the wharf after he left the shipyard, preoccupied as he gazed at the bay. He said, "Someday I want to own a business, perhaps a share in a whaling vessel. It would be a fine change to manage a crew instead of serving on one."
    It pleases me that he has ambition and is planning our future together. However, it might be more encouraging if he had some savings and a dream not involving the whale trade. It makes me nervous when he speaks so wistfully, but he is likely just fatigued. When I walk to the stores in the village here, I miss having a friend waiting for me.

Your friend,
Catherine

Letter from Frank

Division Street
Sag Harbor, New York
January 1, 1848

Dear Cath,
    This year has been the time to get married. I wish you and Michael a joyous new year, as you have set a fashion. Now that Tor and Susie Fee are wed, it has been decided that I am marrying Isabella O'Brien this week. Her brothers have already asked Father McGinnis to perform the ceremony. At least she is charming to behold, even if a bit pensive. After one glance in her direction, the brothers descended on me, demanding my intentions. They have been circling me since they landed in the village from Ireland last year. Maybe Tor and I are not as overprotective

as you thought. The decision happened so fast that we will just have a ceremony with witnesses.

I am sure you are not missing me. Being a married lady must be far preferable to cooking and cleaning for your brother. Speaking of brothers, a letter from Johnny to all of us arrived recently. He is finally ready to leave his other "family" to come here. Our contributions will cover his passage in a shared cabin. I told him not to tarry, but that his employment opportunities may be limited to being a farmhand.

We are all struggling. Shipbuilding in Greenport is doing about as well as wharf labor over this way, which is mighty discouraging. The whaleships are staying out longer and coming back with less. Our dreaded farming is the only occupation that pays sufficient wages. Thus far, I am not ready to give up and till the soil. Take care of yourself, my girl. Please do not let that husband of yours heed the siren call and get back on a whaling vessel.

Yours forever,
Frank

Letter from Susie, in Gaelic

Tomasina Farm
Scuttle Hole Road
Bridgehampton, New York
February 6, 1848

Dear Cath,
You are only a boat ride away in Greenport, but it seems farther. I think about our girlhood adventures as I miss you and feel homesick. What happened at the village well in Mullinclavin when we were young has returned to me. We also said goodbye there in what seems like another lifetime.

It was bold for a seven-year-old to say, "I dare you to climb up and walk around the border of this well." You knew I was afraid, so you climbed up despite me shouting, "Do not go up there. Stop!" You held your arms out for balance as you walked around the rim. After a slight slip, you disappeared down the well. I cannot remember being more frightened as I ran to get your brothers.

When Tor, Frank, and I shouted at you, it was a wonder that the whole townland did not come running. I still can hear your tiny voice from below saying, "Help me," when I was sure you must be dead. Frank untied the rope holding the pail. "Tie this rope around your waist, Cath, and we will pull you up," he said.

The three of us pulled with all our strength. You limped up sideways along the stone wall of the narrow well. You held your head so it would not bump against the wall. When you peeped over the top, the bloody gash on your temple made me scream. Your mam was there in no time. Maybe this memory will ease the feeling of missing each other so much.

Your oldest friend,
Susie

❦

Letter from Catherine, in Gaelic

Fourth Street
Greenport, New York
March 18, 1848

Dear Susie,

I miss you more, dear Susie. I have only one woman to talk to, and though she is my sister-in-law, Ellen, we have little in common. That you are also now my sister-in-law and lifelong best friend makes it even harder not to see you often. The incident at the townland well was a memorable day.

I never told you or anyone that something odd and curious happened to me that day. It might have stayed my secret, but in my longing for your company, I will tell you. What is unusual is that I vividly remember those events, though they happened almost seventeen years ago.

While tumbling down the well, my head hit the sides before I landed in the water at the bottom. Since I could not swim, I sank under the water with my eyes open. I saw the moments of my little life fly by like pages of vivid colored illustrations in a picture book. My time on earth was brief then, but there were many scenes. Everything that happened in my seven-year-old life was expanded and compressed at once.

I fought to the water's surface and clung to a rock jutting from the wall to keep from going under again. My apologies if this sounds confusing, as I do not understand it myself. I was in another world for a while, which is much to ponder for anyone, especially a wee girl.

The events of that day might have remained buried without your prompting. They remind me I had challenges before I ever left home.

Your oldest friend,
Cath

Letter from Catherine

Fourth Street
Greenport, New York
March 24, 1848

Dear Patrick,

I hope enough time has passed for you to have returned to New York. My employment at the Wyandanch Hotel is tolerable, and my new sister-in-law and colleague keeps me company there. I have settled into married life and feel content.

Now I have the acquaintance of another writer in a hotel tavern. Walt Whitman was a boyish, severe fellow with penetrating eyes and an infectious laugh who was instantly memorable. We admired our mutual acquaintance, Herman Melville, as we had each read *Typee* in the last year. He spoke about New York City with such verve that my previous objections softened. Mr. Whitman, who was visiting his sister in Greenport, said he had just returned from a trip to New Orleans. I felt flattered that he asked for tutoring in French, as he learned some phrases there.

He was working on a book of poetry he planned to call *Leaves of Grass*. It prompted me to chuckle at such an improbable, convoluted title. After he had read several poems aloud, their brilliant, biting rawness seared them into my mind. Whitman fairly shouted one line from a poem in the middle of the tavern: "Manhattan's streets I saunter'd pondering." Then he surprised me further by urging me, "Move to Manhattan. You belong there."

It was a curious comment for a staid married lady who had no desire to return there. "I wish you a fine end to your visit and best of luck finishing your book," I replied. Besides you, now I know someone else residing in the metropolis I left behind.

Your penfriend,
Cath

Letter from Catherine, in Gaelic

Fourth Street
Greenport, New York
April 2, 1848

Dear Johnny,

You plan to make your passage soon, but life has undergone an upheaval here. The year 1848 has stunned us with a thunderclap. Gold was discovered in the hills of California. Suddenly, almost every man in the villages of Greenport and Sag Harbor plans to leave for the West. They have taken to calling their departure "the gold rush." Activity in the whale fishery has been diminishing for a while. This new idea spreads like a fever among the seamen, and Michael is also convinced of the promises of gold. I am watching a calamity unfold before my eyes.

What this means for your passage, Johnny, I cannot say. After urging you to come sooner for so long, I am almost relieved you are not a part of this mania. Nothing is like it was only a week ago, which is frightening. I will have Frank and Tor advise you on how to proceed. As farming is probably your intention once here, I pray your plans can continue apace. Still you will find a different village of Sag Harbor from the one we have come to know. The boys will write to you soon.

Your loving sister,
Cath

Letter from Catherine

Fourth Street
Greenport, New York
May 14, 1848

Dear Michael,

I hope you find this letter I left for you at the front desk of the Wyandanch Hotel. This is the first night since our wedding that we have been apart. Your visit to the hotel after our disagreement has been so painful. I cannot imagine how we will endure being separated for months. Maybe we shouted at each other too many times last night, but you are my husband and promised to renounce the sea. Yet you have booked a passage away from me on board another vessel.

I consider a voyage to the Pacific Ocean as going to sea, Michael. We have just begun our marriage, but you will breach our vows if you disappear again. I spent our courtship alone, and I consider it the height of unfairness to spend our young marriage alone. Please do not betray what we promised.

I will get a second job if you think we need more money. I will take in laundry and scrub floors to keep you here. Our extended family is here to help and support our union, no matter what tribulations befall us. There is only your unreliable brother to care what happens to you in the wilds of California. Injury, victimhood, or illness could transpire with no one to rely on, as William would probably leave you behind once again.

Maybe the rush is a lie, and there is little gold to be found. Just because, by hearsay, people believe there are riches for all does not make it so. To go so far after something so ephemeral is a significant risk that has a price. Leaving your wife behind is a step you may regret.

I deserve the married life we promised each other. My brothers warned me I would be left alone. Please do not make their predictions come to pass. If you truly love me, you will not leave me.

Your loving wife,
Cathy

SUSAN MCGUIRK

Letter from Michael

Wyandanch Hotel
Third Street
Greenport, New York
May 15, 1848

Dear Cathy,

I, too, hated being separated last night, but we have been over this subject repeatedly and cannot seem to have a civil conversation. I will put my thoughts on paper so we can try once more to come to an understanding. You have insisted that I stay, reminding me I promised. To remind you, I vowed not to go on a whaling vessel as a crewman. I have no intention of doing so. My word means more than that, and you must trust it. I merely propose that I take a leave from shipbuilding and try my luck for a few months in California.

I will go there as a passenger, not a crew member. It would be less than a year, not years. This is the time to travel there because news of striking gold in California is only beginning to be known. I have advance knowledge from whaling mates who just returned from San Francisco, so my chances of striking gold are better than future competitors. What remains true is that I have promised never to hunt whales again. I need this chance, Cathy. Please try to understand.

Your loving husband,
Michael

Letter from Catherine

Fourth Street
Greenport, New York
May 16, 1848

Dear Michael,

I have used every argument I can think of to implore you to stay, so I give up. Instead, I ask you to take me along. The most important thing is for us to be together. Where we live is a temporary circumstance. As our wedding vows dictate, let me follow you to remain your wife.

I have already boarded a vessel to cross an ocean and can do it again. Hardship and deprivation will not deter me. I have endured them for much of my life, growing up on an impoverished farm. You could consider me your companion and help meet on the voyage, not extra baggage. Once in California, I will find employment and contribute wages as I do now.

Women can go on whaling voyages, as a few captains' wives from Sag Harbor have done. If they were able to successfully navigate the voyage, then so can I to California. Your sister agrees with me. I may even achieve my dream of becoming a teacher in the West, as an accent might not be so off-putting there. If none of my arguments sway you, then I must implore you to have mercy on my plea. If you love me, you cannot flatly refuse me. I am begging, Michael.

Your loving wife,
Cathy

Letter from Michael

Wyandanch Hotel
Third Street
Greenport, New York
May 17, 1848

Dear Cathy,

I have slept very little apart from you, and we must stop arguing and reconcile before I leave. I would be less than a man to subject my wife to the rough conditions among miners in the back hills of California. A cultured lady should not be subjected to such a place. Where I am going not only lacks schools but has no towns or villages. I will sleep in a tent without modern comforts, cooking over a fire under the stars. Clothes may not be changed often and will be washed in a stream. I will be at the mercy of the elements, be they freezing cold, soaking wet, or boiling hot.

We may be miles from a town where you could receive mail from your family. You would be out of touch with them for months. It will be a world inhabited almost exclusively by men. Living primitively, they will behave in kind. I cannot, in good faith or conscience, consider exposing you to such a situation for a moment.

The proposition of the gold rush is too good to resist. There is much to be gained and little to lose. The shipyard is barely surviving, and the last thing I want is to be without a trade. If I remain behind, I will lose my position and be left with nothing. I have already lost one profession. All the lads are going because we will return with gold. It will provide for our lives here for years to come. We must look beyond today to what will benefit us in the future. As the man of our family, I am compelled to go. Please understand, Cathy.

Your loving husband,
Michael

Letter from Frank

Division Street
Sag Harbor, New York
May 21, 1848

Dear Cath,

I understand why Michael is going to California. All the fellows are leaving, too. There is no employment, and we cannot watch our families starve. Since oil was discovered in Pennsylvania, many whaleships have ceased their voyages. It was bad enough that the number of whales was diminishing, but now whale oil prices have plummeted. No wonder the dock is so quiet. I am sorely tempted to go myself, but I cannot leave poor Isabella. She is a frail creature, and my leaving could bring on a spell or worse.

Please try to understand Michael's point of view. I will be left as one of the few able-bodied men still living in the village. Perhaps with all the lads gone, some suitable labor will come to me. I do not blame Michael when hundreds of men from these parts are leaving. You are strong, Cath, my girl, stronger than all of us. You can bear this and continue your life together when he returns.

Yours forever,
Frank

Letter from Michael

67 Greenwich Street
New York City
June 4, 1848

Dear Cathy,

I am staying in an old boarding house before our ship sails to San Francisco later in the week. Please try to understand why I need to leave, like most of the men in our villages. I must provide for you in some fashion. There is no livelihood, and we must accept that fact. I have heard that even in the Arctic whales are dwindling, which means shipbuilding is grinding to a halt. Still we will have a bright future together when I return with bags of gold. Trust me, Cathy, we are going to be rich.

I crossed an ocean to better my luck, and now I will cross the country to do the same. This time, I will do it for both of us. Please be patient, as it will be shorter than a whaling voyage, and I will be home next year. Once in California, we will locate a town near our encampment where letters can be retrieved. I will write with the address. May I implore you to look after Ellen while I am gone? She loves you like a sister, and I promise she will not be a burden.

All my wishes regarding this trip are in service to you. It will improve our life together. I know I am asking you to pay a price. I would not do it if it were not to better our future. It will be difficult for me to be away from you as well. You remain all to me, and I will prevail for us.

All my love,
Michael

SUSAN MCGUIRK

Letter from Tor

Tomasina Farm
Scuttle Hole Road
Bridgehampton, New York
June 20, 1848

Dear Cath,
   I will not say what I think, as it would be cruel. "I told you so" is a phrase with no useful purpose now. However, I want to invite you back to the farm, where you can finally be with your family. As you will see below, there is no better time to reunite than the present.

Your brother,
Tor

   PostScript from Susie:
   Cath, I am in the family way! I need you now more than ever. Please come home soon.

Your oldest friend,
Susie

༄

Letter from Catherine

Fourth Street
Greenport, New York
June 25, 1848

Dear Jane,
   I have heard that the gold rush exodus has struck Sag Harbor as dramatically as Greenport. Michael has already left. He wrote me a parting letter, but rather than reassure me, it left me adrift. Tor and Susie want me to come to the farm. Living with a happy family may only increase my disappointment at being left alone, as much as I love them.
   As I trudge through my duties, the days here serve no purpose without someone to love. A gloom has descended on me that I cannot

escape as time stretches before me. The streets are becoming strangely quiet and unsettling. The only activity at the harbor is whale vessels being refitted for passengers destined for San Francisco.

Fewer visitors are arriving at the hotel, and Ellen and I wonder if we might be dismissed. Since arriving here as a newly wedded wife, I have barely adjusted to living in Greenport. The little house we rented is deadly quiet and remote. I sit, looking out the window at the bay as if I were in another person's life.

I fear being alone in this place after so many dislocations. Yesterday, a fit of anger directed at my husband welled in me. I wailed aloud, "You have left my life asunder, Michael. You said you would not leave me, and I have nothing left. What right did you have to do this to me?" I am sorry for burdening you with my latest bout of self-pity. I hope the migration westward is not adversely affecting you.

Your friend,
Catherine

Letter from Jane

Division Street
Sag Harbor, New York
July 18, 1848

Dear Catherine,

I wanted you to be among the first to know this. I have left Silas, and he will not be my husband anymore. When he found out how much money I saved, he tried to claim it as his own. No one is taking my hard-earned dollars, especially Silas. He had the nerve to put this note in the *Sag Harbor Corrector*: "Whereas my wife, Jane, after robbing my house, has left my bed and board without cause, I do hereby forbid all persons harboring or trusting her. I will pay no debts contracted by her."

He is the one with debts, and I am a woman with money saved. I never told him where I hid it because I feared this might happen. That money is for the house I promised myself I would own someday. It may be on a tiny plot of land, but it will be my castle. I rise above Mr. Mulford because I can see it waiting for me. I will learn to live on my own starting now.

I hope you follow my lead and save your wages. Watching these silly men chase gold shows me we women are all we have. That is why I want you to come back to Sag Harbor. I miss your odd ways, not like anyone else I have met. You tickle me with all your grand sayings, which I learned are your Irish way. They tell me I am a strange one, but when they made you, the spirits stirred the pot backward.

You mustn't be away from your family, over there alone in Greenport. Also, thank you for saying nice things about my writing. Coming from an almost teacher, I am pleased. Our Montaukett tribe has long cared about learning, even for girls. My group of books has grown to almost half a dozen, which I will share with you. I have *The Last of the Mohicans* and the Bible. Come back home because your stewing and fretting will have run wild by now.

Your friend,
Jane

Letter from Catherine

Fourth Street
Greenport, New York
July 21, 1848

Dear Patrick,

Forgive my desolation. I am indeed married to a dreamer. Michael believes he will become rich in the gold rush and has departed. That most men from this and surrounding villages have also left gives me no succor. Nothing changes the fact that I am alone and uncertain.

I forced myself to be patient, having spent our entire courtship alone. However, my tolerance is exhausted, as I never thought marriage would also mean solitude. Has the fever struck you? You seem too sensible to become caught up in the frenzy. Then again, the address you left is a route to the gold rush. Of course, you were doing business in Central America before, so perhaps you have risen above the mania. I look forward to hearing your response.

Your penfriend,
Catherine

Letter from Patrick

San Juan del Norte
Nicaragua
August 29, 1848

Dear Catherine,

I am sorry that you are suffering. Many of the young men in New York have also absconded to California. In my case, there is no fever, but there is an opportunity. I, too, am involved in the gold rush, but as a provider of transportation to California, not a prospector.

Mr. Vanderbilt started a firm called The Accessory Transit Company, which I manage. We transport would-be miners from the East Coast to San Juan del Norte, a Nicaraguan city near the Caribbean side. From there, the trip goes by riverboat to the town of Rivas. Then, one catches a short stagecoach ride to the coast, where a steamboat transports our passengers to San Francisco. Our itinerary is cheaper and shorter than the sea or overland routes.

You are alone and bereft, and I feel partly responsible. I was unavailable as a devoted friend. If I had not been busy hacking through a jungle, perhaps I could have made a difference. Now, I am still not the friend you need in a time of suffering, but my plea remains the same. If you ever want to change your life, I will reverse course and come to your side. What if you refrained from asking yourself, "Would I be wrong to leave?" Instead, I could offer, "Whatever challenges leaving would incur, we could solve the dilemmas on our way together."

I am wildly speculating, but please do not dismiss my ranting out of hand. Perhaps you can keep it in the back of your mind for diversion, if nothing else. At least I have the means now. Nothing could be more rewarding for me than to offer you respite in any capacity. We are already making a tidy profit, and the business is growing monthly.

As for a ray of hope, the possibility exists that some miners will make a decent return in the rush. Indeed, many thousands believe in their chances. Maybe your husband, one of the earliest miners to go, will be one of them.

Your penfriend,
Patrick

SUSAN MCGUIRK

❧

Letter from Susie, in Gaelic

Tomasina Farm
Scuttle Hole Road
Bridgehampton, New York
August 31, 1848

Dear Cath,

You are hearing from a new mother! Francis was born a few days ago, and we are both doing well. Thank you for heeding your family's wishes and returning to Sag Harbor from Greenport. Being so close, you can visit Francis and me soon. My little darling cannot wait to meet his Aunt Cath. I know you are struggling with life on your own, as so many women we know are. Please remember I am here whenever you need me.

Your oldest friend,
Susie

❧

Letter from Catherine, in Gaelic

Division Street
Sag Harbor, New York
September 28, 1848

Dear Susie,

I am thrilled to report that little Francis has a cousin on the way! I suspected as much when I visited you, but the midwife has confirmed it. This is the most beautiful blessing of my life. I can hardly wait for Michael to return to share it with him. My darling child will never want for anything. I will do everything in my power to make my little angel happy and healthy. My turn has finally come, and my life will never be the same. In the meantime, I will depend on you as Francis's new mother to guide me.

I feel relief and joy at being finished with Greenport, as I missed my family more than I admitted. Jane is pleased to have her old neighbor back. The village is increasingly empty, with so many men fleeing to the gold rush. I felt guilty about leaving Ellen behind and offered for her to accompany me, but she is content to keep boarding with her fellow chambermaids for now.

Living in my old room at Frank's small house is better than expected. Maybe my presence is a little snug for a married couple like Isabella and Frank, but they welcome my share of the rent now that I have returned to employment at the Nassau Hotel. As Isabella is with child as well, they are saving every penny.

Frank's bride has had trouble adjusting to married life, maybe because she endured the famine directly. I secretly wonder if her brothers were so overprotective to hide her strange ways, especially from Frank. Maybe they knew that Isabella's beauty, not her conversation, would lead to a successful courtship.

I have tried to befriend and help her, but she is usually vague. Her responses to questions are frequently unexpected, either too abrupt or trailing off unfinished. Her organizational and cooking skills in the house are lacking, something I forgive as mine are, too. My domestic abilities, however, are deficient from a lack of interest, while she aspires, unsuccessfully, to master them. Everything has improved since we will be mothers together, months apart, within the year. This may be a chance for us to become more like sisters.

We are helping each other with our preparations, as we both have difficulties with our delicate conditions. I have always considered myself strong and hearty, but losing my breakfast and sometimes dinner day after day is wearisome. So far, I can conceal my condition from the hotel. I do not want to lose my wages any sooner than needed. Unfortunately, standing on my feet all day is not helping.

Poor Isabella's situation is worse, as she has been confined to bed and is quite helpless. At least I have my meek little friend to share impending motherhood with during Michael's absence. If not for having a daily compatriot, I might go a bit mad. Frank is sympathetic, but he is busy tending to Isabella's incapacity. On my next day at liberty from the hotel, I will walk over to see you. I have many questions for an experienced mother like yourself.

Your oldest friend,
Cath

SUSAN MCGUIRK

Letter from Susie, in Gaelic

Tomasina Farm
Scuttle Hole Road
Bridgehampton, New York
October 15, 1848

Dear Cath,
After your visit, I would not be truthful if I had said you seemed well. You are not gaining the weight you should be due to all your stomach sickness. I wish you would come to the farm and spend your confinement here. There is more room to settle in, and I could help you. You could practice holding baby Francis, and we could prepare together. Something is not right, and I am worried about you. It could be your coloring is too pale. It may be the way you bend to the left and become out of breath. Please come here by my side, Cath. It would quiet my mind.

Your oldest friend,
Susie

Letter from Catherine, in Gaelic

Division Street
Sag Harbor, New York
October 22, 1848

Dear Susie,
Isabella gave birth to little Mamie yesterday. Her arrival only increases my anticipation of my turn at the joys of motherhood in a few months. I still cannot believe that Michael has a complete lack of knowledge about my condition. I await his arrival home next year to our new life as the parents of a beautiful baby.
Letters have been slow to arrive here for anyone from California. According to the few reports in the *Sag Harbor Corrector*, life there sounds primitive and isolated. People live in rural encampments without names, much less postal service. Few families have received addresses in California to correspond with. I must be patient like the women here

who give birth with their husbands away at sea. I will summon my courage and put on a brave front. Still, I wish I could write to Michael with our joyous news and not have this interminable wait.

I have put off telling you this since I started this letter, but something is bothering me, Susie. I do not have the words to explain it. There is an odd sensation that my insides feel like they are sinking. I do not know what is wrong with me, but I will come to you soon.

Your oldest friend,
Cath

Letter from Catherine

Tomasina Farm
Scuttle Hole Road
Bridgehampton, New York
January 12, 1849

Dear Michael,
From birth, our child's life quickly failed due to what the midwife described as "weakness." After a couple of hours, on January 10, God took our baby to heaven. I did not have the heart to give her a name. The line on the record the midwife filled out for the Town of Southampton remained empty, like everything inside me. Part of my soul has died along with our daughter. I feel nothing and no longer care about myself, you, or anyone else. I want to lie down and sleep for a long time, maybe forever. You are not here.

Your wife,
Cathy

SUSAN MCGUIRK

Letter from Catherine

Tomasina Farm
Scuttle Hole Road
Bridgehampton, New York
January 13, 1849

Dear Jane,
 I wrote to Michael about our baby dying. I opened my wedding hope chest and took out my lace wedding handkerchief. I wrapped a tiny lock of hair from my baby daughter inside it. My wedding ring slid off my finger, and I placed it inside, as well. The envelope of money I had saved at your behest was withdrawn. The chest creaked as the key turned in the lock. I watched as the letter I wrote to Michael rose in flames in my washbasin.

Your friend,
Catherine

Letter from Jane

Division Street
Sag Harbor, New York
January 16, 1849

Dear Catherine,
 I am writing this because some stories are too hard to tell, sitting side by side. Death is a poor subject when you are still mourning, as I am in Silas's passing. We were still fighting when he died. Now that he is gone, I see our spat meant so little.
 I never told you this, but I lost two babies at birth, Mary Elizabeth and Edward. Your pain of losing a daughter is mine. I always thought of myself as strong. I accepted anything the spirits sent me, but those losses wore out my soul. I could not rise out of the bed, Catherine. Days of my life went by, and Silas kept asking what was wrong with me. I could see his mouth moving, but I could not hear him.
 My hole was so deep that I gave up hope of ever digging out. I had a dream where a strange child came and told me to dig the hole even

deeper. I asked her after each dig, "Is this deep enough?" but she kept shaking her head no. Finally, she said, "Keep digging until you reach the bottom of your soul. When you get there, you will be delivered."

This is when we of the Algonquin peoples know the spirits speak to us in dreams. The messages can be shown not just through other people but by animals or stories from nature. They bond you to the Great Spirit, those who come before, nature, and our path. A nightmare may be a warning or a test. The messages may be a sign of what is to come. Someday I will explain how, but my message saved me. Let the spirits speak to you now in your dreams. They will save you, too.

The children we brought forth and our time as mothers have gone to the spirits. They led us to each other to help heal the pain of our lost ones. The children came, and we knew them, if only for a little while. That is our bond, Catherine, made of bone and sinew. When we go beyond, we will braid our daughters' hair into plaits. They will weave a story of how our fiber connects to each other, our peoples, and our hearts. When the strands of mind, body, and spirit are braided together, there is a harmony that makes us strong. That is the feeling we must reach for all our lives on our way home.

Your friend,
Jane

Letter from Catherine

Tomasina Farm
Scuttle Hole Road
Bridgehampton, New York
February 1, 1849

Dear Jane,

The spirits are as silent as my heart. I called them, but there was no answer. I cannot dig deeper because I am already at the bottom. The sight of a tiny baby's lifeless body covered with a cloth haunts me. They pulled me off her as I screamed and tried to clutch her back. "You cannot have her! She must stay with me even if she is dead," I shrieked at them. Susie dragged me away from her with the midwife's help. I remember very little after that. They buried my baby in Saint Andrew's Cemetery, but I was not there. I do not know where I was.

I cannot find God. I do not want to be here anymore. This is not my home. I have nowhere to go. I want to be with my baby, with Mam and Da. There is no place for me here. I do not know anyone any longer except you. All the rest are strangers. My husband is a stranger. I am here only because of your words. They are the only reason I have not followed my baby. Thank you for that rope to hold on to.

After I gave birth, they thought I was dying from blood loss. I felt myself at the bottom of a well I had been in before. The moments of my life passed before me as years were mysteriously condensed into seconds, each moment perfectly distinct. When it stopped, light enveloped me in perfect peace. Seconds later, I returned to true desolation. There was no way back to the bliss I had crossed into. I was lying on a bed, but it felt like being trapped inside a bottomless well.

Your friend,
Catherine

Letter from Jane

Division Street
Sag Harbor, New York
February 15, 1849

Dear Catherine,

The spirits are with you. The place they sent you to in the light is their home. They tell you it is not your time to join them, but they will help you find your path. Do not lose heart, Catherine. The spirits spoke to you, and you heard them, so you are not alone. Give yourself time to heal and then stand up and go where they send you.

Your friend,
Jane

Letter from Catherine

Tomasina Farm
Scuttle Hole Road
Bridgehampton, New York
February 20, 1849

Dear Jane,

For days, I stayed alone in the spare room at the farm. I finally emerged to have a meal with my family. The only words that I can grasp are yours. I am unsure what they mean, but a door has closed. I can no longer dwell among these thriving families in a place that only reminds me of my previous happiness. The burning desire to go to Saint Andrew's Cemetery has receded. I no longer wish to crawl into the hole in the ground with my baby. If I cannot return to my previous self, I must invent someone new. It must be someone without a heart so it cannot be broken into little pieces, someone far away from here.

A couple of nights ago, a line from a poem Walt Whitman worked on in Greenport came back to me: "Manhattan's streets I saunter'd pondering." When I woke up, I tried to remember whether I had heard a message in my dreams. I remembered nothing. Though, once awake, the words Mr. Whitman placed in my head resounded like a piano tune. I fell asleep that night with his persistent voice in my ear and woke up with it like a refrain: "Manhattan's streets I saunter'd pondering."

The words from the past became the present, as I found the release you described. It was from this place that I thought was my home to where the poem sent me, New York City. I will return to a coarsened city with my hardened heart, no longer able to feel anything, even fear.

As I clutched my pendant of Princess Erca, I summoned her from her grave on the Island of Iona off the coast of Scotland, buried over a thousand years ago. I implored, "Send me the fortitude I lack to take one step forward. I must rise at this moment and forge a course of action, or I will be condemned to ignominy forever."

I shakily stood up to gather my possessions to return to Frank's house to prepare to leave for good. The railroad was my wings to Sag Harbor. I would step aboard it again to salvage the last remnants of my life. I stared at the stranger in the mirror. She coldly stated, "New York is a place that defeated me once, but now I have nothing left to lose."

Your friend,
Catherine

Letter from Jane

Division Street
Sag Harbor, New York
February 26, 1849

Dear Catherine,
I am releasing you to call upon me. It seems the spirits want me to guide you for a spell. You said we are fated to be friends, and it appears true now. You may be afraid you will ask too much, but we cannot argue with what is. Experience, pain, sorrow, and trust tie us to each other. Call upon me, and I will answer.

Your friend,
Jane

> Sail forth! steer for the deep waters only!
> Reckless, O soul, exploring, I with thee, and thou with me;
> For we are bound where mariner has not yet dared go,
> And we will risk the ship, ourselves and all.
>
> "Passage to India," 13
> *Leaves of Grass*
> Walt Whitman

Chapter Four

1849–1851

Letter from Susie, in Gaelic

Tomasina Farm
Scuttle Hole Road
Bridgehampton, New York
March 2, 1849

Dear Cath,

    I cannot say which is worse, my sadness I am losing you again or my fear for you in New York. I pray the grief in your heart fades. You are not yourself and are in no condition to go anywhere, especially to a crude and dangerous place. I cannot lessen your pain, as all mothers, deep inside, question whether they can survive what God has sent you. We are only human and have limits, but I know you. I cannot imagine you being defeated. If you say you must move to New York, I will not try to stop you. Part of me always knew you would not stay with me.

    Our lives are moving in different directions. Your future is unknown, but I am a farmer's wife, and will continue to be. I know what time to get up each day and go to sleep. My chores are laid out for me. This is the life I wanted, but one that would have made you unhappy. You are different not just from me, but from the girls we grew up with. Most of them probably became farmers' wives, too. There is only one Cath. I understand you must be true to yourself.

    I will do anything to help, but I still wish you would stay close. All my roving got used up crossing the sea to be with you. I would ask you to think again, Cath, but I know you, so I will not waste my breath. Farewell, my dearest.

Your oldest friend,
Susie

༄

Letter from Catherine, in Gaelic

Division Street
Sag Harbor, New York
April 16, 1849

Dear Susie,

I know what you are trying to do, and I thank you for the effort. I will go on, but you must accept me as I am now. Though I will always be your Cath, my soul belongs to a stranger named Catherine. My life must never be threatened again. To shield myself from that fate, I will do whatever is required. I will survive, but not like the girl you ran down the hill with. I must protect myself by banishing Michael from my future.

He left me to suffer death, grief, and despair alone. I cannot afford to be in that position again, as I would not endure it twice. You may think me harsh and unforgiving, but there is no choice. My life and prospects depend on it. I can never, for any reason, go back to those dreadful days.

It was bad enough that Michael was absent, but he did not know what happened and had no way of finding out. He made the choice to disappear from our life together, from me. I refuse to live with that choice. He left me, and now I am leaving him. I am not the little woman, the waiting wife, or the whaling widow. I am Catherine alone. It is no wonder if you do not understand, Susie. I only hope you can accept your friend as she is now.

Your oldest friend,
Cath

Letter from Susie, in Gaelic

Tomasina Farm
Scuttle Hole Road
Bridgehampton, New York
May 1, 1849

Dear Cath,
    You may not remember all that happened, Cath, but I was there. We almost lost you, in body and mind. I am happy you returned to us, but I know you are different. You are my oldest friend and now sister through marriage, and I will always love and accept the woman you are. We were always different, and that has not changed. We each have our place in each other's lives and hearts.
    I always wanted to be like my friend Cath. You are a fighter, which is something I will never be. We have different natures, and neither of us can follow the path of the other. We would fail if we tried. I will stay where I am, at the spinning wheel, the laundry basket, the milking stool, and the cradle. I learned the story of your hero, Joan of Arc, in hedge school. You must take up the "Sword of Catherine" that she carried into battle. Only then will you take your proper name in full. Still, you will always be Cath to me.

Your oldest friend,
Susie

Letter from Isabella, left on the bureau, in Gaelic

Division Street
Sag Harbor, New York
June 6, 1849

Dear Cath,
    I am afraid Frank will hear me if I try to explain what happened, so I am writing instead. Every word I say irritates him. If he knew what I was

about to tell you, he would be furious. He does not love me and only married me because my brothers made him.

What seemed like a dream last night turned out to be real. I heard a faint voice in my ear whispering my name over and over. I got up and went down the hall, where I saw a little girl. She was wearing a fancy pink pinafore over a white flowing gown, standing in a shining cloud of light. I was afraid at first, but she came and sat on my lap and sang to me. She said her name was Angelina, and she was visiting from heaven.

I hope you do not think I am ranting, Cath. I never went on about the fairies and little people back in the old country, like so many. This is not a story because it happened. I asked Angelina if she had a message for you. She said, "Tell Mama I miss her and will wait for her on the other side." That was all, and then she was gone. I had to tell you, no matter what Frank thinks. Men cannot understand that motherhood is eternal. I am sure you will cherish what I wrote and be happy.

Your sister-in-law,
Isabella

Letter from Catherine, left in the cradle, in Gaelic

Division Street
Sag Harbor, New York
June 7, 1849

Dear Isabella,

I will leave you with this message as I depart for New York. Thank you for telling me your story, and I promise not to tell Frank. I hope you take good care of yourself and Mamie. Frank is devoted to you, and you should not worry so much. Please take time to rest and mend from your confinement. You will need all your strength to be a mother.

I ask you to examine yourself, and think about who you were before you became a wife and mother. See if you can find that beautiful young girl back in County Mayo. Hold fast to that other Isabella, and she will carry you through these trying days. She is the key to your present and future. Frank is there to help you with every step of the journey. Thank you for your recognition of who I am in spirit.

Your sister-in-law,
Cath

Letter from Catherine, left in the shed

Division Street
Sag Harbor, New York
June 7, 1849

Dear Jane,
　I am already calling on your offer of help with this sad note that I will share only with you. My poor sister-in-law, Isabella, has suffered leave of her senses. She wrote me a letter saying my dead child appeared to her. At least she confided in me. I knew I was reading the musings of a woman increasingly estranged from reality. How tragic that such a comely, promising woman has deteriorated into a world of dreams.
　Isabella's letter was indeed shocking. In some small way, it was also consoling. She associated me with motherhood when no one else has but you. In my secret heart, I still see myself as a mother, although of a departed one, but a mother just the same. In this respect, Isabella was right, despite her raving. She said I would understand, and that motherhood is eternal.

Your friend,
Catherine

SUSAN MCGUIRK

Letter from Catherine

Division Street
Sag Harbor, New York
June 8, 1849

Dear Michael,
 This letter will never be sent, as I do not possess an address in the hills of California to which you have fled in the gold rush. Yet I must write to move forward. I do not hate you. Our marriage must be concluded for other reasons, the foremost of which is that there is no marriage. I have no husband.
 You are not here, and I am alone. I am beholding the situation with clarity and honesty. The time has come to stop exerting time and energy fretting over your absence. The sooner I embark on a fresh start for myself, the better. My life had become one of waiting for you to return, to respond, to care, to be.
 That chapter has ended, along with my life's dearest desire, motherhood. I now release forever its promise of hope and happiness. Now that I have seen what lies beyond, I am grateful to be on this side of the divide. Being alive is what I have left, something far from nothing. To breathe and to walk are my new ambitions. I may learn to laugh, to run, to feel, to love again. They are but dreams now, but I will not forget that they were once my life. There is no more, and I bid you farewell, Michael.

Your wife,
Cathy

Letter from Catherine, left in the shed

Division Street
Sag Harbor, New York
June 8, 1849

Dear Jane,
 You said, "We are tied to one another," so I continue to seek your solace. I wrote Michael ending our marriage and threw the letter into

the sea, watching it melt into pieces. My goal is to move to New York alone, but there is a problem. I promised Michael I would watch over his sister, Ellen. As painful a reminder of him as she is, a promise is a promise. I implored Ellen to go to New York with me. She does not know I lost a baby, and I cannot bear to tell her.

I could not wait for Ellen to agree to the trip to prepare. To help propel us forward, I put an advertisement in a New York newspaper for a governess and a housemaid. So far, there have been no responses. Increasingly nervous, I again entreated Ellen and she revealed the real reason for her hesitation. She said, "I, too, am tired of waiting for Michael's return, and your reasons for wanting to start a new life make sense to me. Still, we need to decide how we will speak of my brother in our day-to-day lives." I wait in fear for Ellen to state her requirements. At this most painful juncture, without you as my confidant, Jane, I would fail before I started.

Your grateful friend,
Catherine

Letter from Ellen Heffernan, in Gaelic

Wyandanch Hotel
Third Street
Greenport, New York
June 10, 1849

Dear Cath,
Now that you understand I cannot turn my back on my brother, I will move to New York City with you. Look for me at the station on Thursday. I wish things between the two of you were better, but no one from the outside knows what happens in a marriage. You must have your reasons. I trust they are fair and not bitter, like the Cath I know. Still the Mike I know is not like that either.

There is no brother or parent to ask permission to leave and nothing to hold me here in Greenport. I will try not to fail you in this new life. Mike also left me alone here. With my employment ending, I will leave with you because I have nowhere else to go. As my sister by marriage, you are the only family I have left. If my parents were still alive, I would give up and go back to Ireland. I never thought I would end up left behind.

If I get any word from him, I will still give Mike my Greenport address. I made plans with the post office to forward his letters to New York. I also have a wish in return. Please do not speak ill of him to me. We can stop speaking of him at all if that will help us get along. Thank you for this chance, Cath, but if I had any other place to go, I would not choose this. I owe you a debt I will repay each day with this vow: "I promise not to tell my brother that I live with his wife."

Your almost sister,
Ellen

Letter from Catherine

155 Hudson Street
New York City
July 21, 1849

Dear Frank,

Our saga since leaving Sag Harbor has been harrowing but has a happy ending. Ellen and I arrived in Manhattan without an interview procured. I had one month's worth of boarding house payment in my pocket, thanks to Jane, who urged me to save for myself. The advertisement I placed before I left continued to appear in the newspaper, but no responses came. We knocked on the doors of kitchens in fine houses requesting employment, only to have them unceremoniously shut. Our suitable dresses became splashed with mud and grime. Our shoes became worn through from trudging many miles as opportunities dwindled.

The boarding house, already questionably appropriate for unaccompanied women, tried to extort more rent from us. The neighborhood had not improved from our previous visit and, if anything, had worsened. Like last time, we dodged pickpockets, brazen men, and careening carriages. The long walks to the better neighborhoods to knock on doors left us worn out. The tally of door closings was proportional to our increasing nervousness.

Just as we contemplated retreat to Sag Harbor, the newspaper sent word of a response. We secured an interview in the house of a well-to-do French family, the Bechets. Ellen was offered the position of a housemaid. Once opposite Mr. and Mrs. Bechet, I pressed for the title of governess in French. They said, "We will consider the title of governess if you agree to come alone." As tempted as I was to forget my promise, I insisted, "Ellen and I are a pair." I was promptly demoted to nurse, a bitter setback.

When they asked about Mr. Heffernan's whereabouts, I instinctively lied that he was lost at sea. I told myself there was an element of truth, as he was indeed lost to me. Despite the uncertain start, at least my concerns for safety and protection in the big city dissipated. We live in an impressive mansion in a refined neighborhood, though our rooms are small and plain.

Fortunately, my assignment to teach the children does not require any household labor. This is indeed a monumental leap from my hotel duties. In my precarious state, I must appreciate my professional accomplishments. My long-held ambition of teaching children has come true, even without the designation of the title of governess. Of course, no one could construe a nurse's duty as tutoring children in English language studies. I am also asked to instruct in French and English literature. Still I am flattered that they entrust me with these responsibilities, demonstrating their respect for my expertise. I must derive any semblance of pride I can muster to succeed in this challenge.

The boys have a male tutor, who also lives with the family, to teach mathematics, science, and history. Despite my best efforts at gratitude, it still rankles me. I have the expertise to teach those subjects even though I have far fewer advantages than Mr. Fenton, my rival. He enjoys lording his supposed superior education over mine. Still, he usually comes up short when we are head-to-head, recalling a quotation or verse. "Mrs. Heffernan, how quaint that you know the title of Herman Melville's book *Typee*."

"Yes, Mr. Fenton," I replied, "Mr. Melville had just finished it when we met." That subdued him for a while.

At least my diminished title leaves me more time to dote on my darling Delphina, three years old. As one who loves to sing, dance, and pretend to be various animals, she is a balm to my soul. Her infectious laugh and sunny little disposition illuminate the darkness inside me. Sorry, dear brother, to wax over my tribulations. I hope they do not hinder your pleasant image of your sister, as you are my trusted liege. I send my love to you and your beautiful family.

Yours forever,
Cath

Letter from Susie, in Gaelic

Tomasina Farm
Scuttle Hole Road
Bridgehampton, New York
September 18, 1849

Dear Cath,

You will be happy to know that you now have another niece. Little Minnie and her mama are doing well, though a bit tired. Luckily, she is a sweet, calm baby, as Francis is still a handful. Once the children are asleep, my thoughts can quiet long enough to write a letter. Between Gaelic words, I will try to add new English words Tor has taught me. I am so glad you and Ellen are settled with the Bechet family. I always knew your French would lead you to better places.

Please do not stew. The family will see your teaching skills and, in time, promote you to their governess. In the meantime, nurse duties are not beneath you. If only Michael had not yoked you like an ox to his sister, Ellen. Her common ways did not help your chances of showing your employers how educated you are. She is like an anvil you must haul behind you. You did not ask for or deserve the duty, but at least she is company to you.

As for local gossip, the big news is that some of my recently arrived cousins have found employment in their former trade. They say that when one door closes, another door opens. Back home, they had to stop sending the yarn they spun to Belfast when the York Street Mill closed during the famine. Once they arrived here, the newly opened Steam

Cotton Mill in Sag Harbor hired them. The wages are decent until they can begin farming.

My aunt Bridget had never seen a factory. She expected to impress them with her old-fashioned skills of scutching, bleaching, and beetling. Instead, they wanted her to stand on her feet all day, pulling and pushing machinery. The new world found itself in quite a row with the old country's ways, but progress won. After much hollering, poor old Biddy learned a modern way to spin, and her skills of the past were no longer needed.

As you may have guessed, I am trying to be cheerful. That does not mean I have stopped worrying about you in that rough place. I still wish that you were here on the farm, but I am glad little Delphina has come into your life. She may be the perfect answer to these past months, which is a comfort.

Your oldest friend,
Susie

Letter from Catherine

155 Hudson Street
New York City
December 17, 1849

Dear Patrick,

I am sorry I have not answered your last letter until now. I waited, as I knew you would already be gone to Nicaragua. Your "ranting" has helped me survive some tumultuous times. As you can see from my return address, I now live in our original destination. As I continue to burden you with my problems, I hope you will not regret your kind offer of penfriendship. Your stories are so exciting and hopeful, and mine are just the opposite.

I listen to the din of the Hudson River Railroad being built in the distance. Longing for quiet, I dream about the stillness of our farm in Mullinclavin. I am sure your townland was much the same. We were never lonely there, with every inhabitant knowing our names and family. Everyone was like us, with no possibility of anyone looking askance or detecting an accent. Home was where verdant valleys of gossamer mist soothed nerves and worries. We gathered around a warm hearth with our loving family. It could not erase the worry of the tax bill, but we could forget for one night.

Now, I am a stranger to all I pass, someone they probably do not notice or remember. Bustling Sag Harbor is a rural respite compared to this seething metropolis. Where I am employed as a nurse, my small room is my refuge. I can become lost in my books at night in the quiet. Reading to my charge, Delphina, each night while her little blond curls fall across my shoulder is the culmination of my day. Her sweet, trusting eyes gazing into mine soothe my soul. For now, my small world of teaching French children is enough for me to march through the days. It may be one tiny step at a time, but I am grateful.

The Bechet house is on Hudson Street, bordering a bucolic retreat named Saint John's Park. Across the park is Saint John's Chapel, an Episcopal church that is usually locked but has melodic bells that chime regularly. From my corner window facing the park, I have found my old friend Walt Whitman's directives. During my daily visits with the children, I remember his musings on nature as a balm to my spirit.

Now, I bring him up with trepidation. This new version of New York matches his words better than the one I first encountered with you. "I swear I see now that every thing has an eternal soul! The trees have, rooted in the ground! the weeds of the sea have! the animals!" As I stroll through the wooded landscape, I contemplate the flowers, the birds, and the ever-present emptiness inside me. You see, Patrick, I lost a baby in childbirth when I was alone. I ran as far away as I could, but the terrible void followed me here.

Your penfriend,
Catherine

Letter from Patrick

San Juan del Norte
Nicaragua
March 24, 1850

Dear Catherine,
   I offer you my sincerest condolences upon the loss of your child. I

will keep you in my heart and my prayers. Your suffering is very painful for me to contemplate. Part of me wants to quit my job and run to you. I am so distressed that I cannot ease your suffering.

The idea I am about to suggest may appear outlandish, but I mean every word. Please do not consider this a last resort to rescue you. This proposition is a sincere, well-reasoned, and heartfelt effort to benefit us both. As I am not present, please imagine that I am on one knee, holding your hand, looking up at you with this request.

"Please come to Nicaragua and agree to be my wife. Let us build a new life and future here together where no one will question our past or present. I will teach you the language and customs, and we will never look back. You need only say yes, and I will take care of everything."

You know how much I have longed for this chance. I know it would be unlikely for you to agree, but I hope you truly consider my second marriage proposal. As I will explain, we would have the means to live a safe, comfortable life of freedom and happiness.

Just as small towns in California are thriving due to the influx of the forty-niners, so is the town of San Juan del Norte. Every imaginable type of person is bustling through, most trying to make their way to the gold rush. New York may still be foreign to you, but spending time in San Juan del Norte would be a larger adjustment. Yet for those of us who choose this way station as a destination, our fortunes are flourishing. As a boy in hedge school, I learned about the rise of the Roman Empire. Now I find myself in the middle of a tiny version of it.

Our business, The Accessory Transit Company, is growing with great velocity. We strive to serve the thousands vying for our services to transport them to San Francisco. I marvel that my salary continues to climb with the company's fortunes. If the pace of growth continues, I can consider myself a successful man of business.

It would be my honor to offer you a secure life. From my deep knowledge and experience of the system here, I believe we would be immune from all scrutiny or curiosity. You would be Mrs. Lynch, a woman above reproach or inquiry.

If you consider this a flight of fancy, I promise to remain on the periphery where I belong. As difficult as propriety can sometimes be to maintain, I would never want to compromise your standing. However, please know that should anything change, I will fly to your side.

I have an inkling of your loneliness as I continue to be a single man. The answer for me is to keep traveling to both coasts from Nicaragua. There is no time for reflection or a permanent home to miss. When I travel to San Francisco for Mr. Vanderbilt, I gape at the raw enterprise whirling around me. For a few days, it is an exciting diversion before taking my leave. Mr. Vanderbilt also recently sent me to Jamaica, a fascinating place.

With a snap of your fingers, you can convert my wandering into settling down with you. We will dwell in a sprawling hacienda, in a life of love and leisure. The offer to change your destiny stands for as long as our bond endures.

Your penfriend,
Patrick

Letter from Frank

Division Street
Sag Harbor, New York
March 25, 1850

Dear Cath,

I am always ready and eager to receive a message from my dear sister. A few letters from Michael have come and gone back, as mail takes months from the mining camps of California. I have heard the lads live in tents in the mountains, if they are lucky enough to have them. I hate to say it because, as you know, Michael was not my favorite, but I feel sorry for him. I respect your wishes to return the letters, so there is no need to get upset with me.

Fatherhood is my pleasure, but it requires more than I anticipated, as Isabella slowly slips away. She and her brothers left a different Ireland than we did. They came because they were evicted from their land in the famine and were nearly starving. By the time they arrived, no wonder they were all so untrusting and protective.

Once I was married to Isabella, I could see that she lacked the resiliency of most Irish folk. It may be because she is slight in build, frequently sick, and can barely withstand hardship.

She still has good days when all is fine, which gives me hope. For now, sometimes, we remain a happy family on Division Street. However, apart from Isabella's troubles, wages are increasingly hard to earn here. With labor becoming scarce, I, too, am hearing the siren call of gold.

Yours forever,
Frank

Letter from Tor

Tomasina Farm
Scuttle Hole Road
Bridgehampton, New York
March 27, 1850

Dear Cath,

Please understand that I support your aims. Even so, it puzzles and surprises me that you believed the Bechet family would assign you the role of a governess. We both understand that our family is as good as any and that we can hold our heads up with the best of them. However, people of the breeding, refinement, and wealth of your employers would not let an Irish immigrant teach their children in that capacity. This is only reasonable, Cath.

You were a better student than I was in school, but I am not talking about book learning. Your French is excellent, but as you know, there is a prejudice that we Irish are subject to, especially in New York City. They will simply not see you in a professional capacity. Please do not be disheartened by my frankness. I do not want you to be disappointed by wishing for something you will not receive.

I must implore you one more time to return home to your family. We will never see our homeland or parents again; may they rest in peace. We are all in this country, but our sister, whom we love, is not among us. You do not belong in the world alone, especially in an enormous, threatening city. No woman cherished by her family should be in such a position. Please come home as soon as possible. I am concerned about you.

Your brother,
Tor

SUSAN MCGUIRK

Letter from Catherine

155 Hudson Street
New York City
April 30, 1850

Dear Tor,

 I try to soften the sting of your candor by telling myself that you were only trying to be the man of the family, though it appears somewhat misguided to me. I understand you carry the heavy burden of responsibility for us all in this new world. However, you demeaned my efforts and thwarted my ambition. Believe it or not, we ladies can have aspirations, or perhaps the word hope is more palatable to you. I believe such a sentiment is not illegal or against the Ten Commandments. I sincerely hope you have not fainted, dear brother.

 It will be difficult to forget your harsh summation of my decisions and deportment. I must guide my life and determine my actions, wishes, and dreams. They remain despite the wayward turns of my life. Please do not judge me, Tor. When someone has lost their husband, their home, their child, and their hope, only God can judge them.

 I will never regret marrying for love, as if I had a choice. It would be intolerable to be a prisoner in a home with a man who has no feelings for me. It would be worse if I had none for him. Let me spend my days teaching my charges, seeing their young minds expand while I use my own.

 As someone who knows my nature, you cannot expect me to be otherwise. You encouraged me to climb trees and race you down the hill. You fought for me to attend the Irish Society School and labor at the castle. I am still the same Cath, though a battle-worn version of her. Please stop expecting me to change the disposition I was born with, Tor. My life might have been easier being pliable and agreeable, but that was not ordained for me. I can hear you now: "You could always cajole me into agreeing with you." I am making my case because I value your opinion.

 Before you throw my letter down in disgust, please remember you are the only person I trusted to step onto the gangway of the ship *Queen Victoria*. We stuck together through the streets of New York, the railroad days, and the early time in Sag Harbor. While we may be apart, we are still in proximity to each other and still one family.

Your loving sister,
Cath

༝

Letter from Catherine

155 Hudson Street
New York City
May 15, 1850

Dear Patrick,

 I have never been so touched and grateful by the caring of another. Your letter came at a time of uncertainty and sadness and has gone far in healing my aching heart. That is why it makes it more painful to be in the position of refusing your proposal for the second time. I simply lack the courage to entertain such a venture. When no one in Nicaragua knew we were not truly husband and wife, I would know. It would be impossible to reconcile the guilt and fear of living a life of untruth. Also, my ties to my family would have to be severed, which is something I could never do.

 Yet flying into your arms is all I want. Just knowing of the possibility has solidified my existence. I am more attuned to my present circumstances and not so much like a stranger trudging through the masquerade of living. Knowing that somewhere in the world, someone cherishes me makes the quotidian endurable and even sometimes pleasurable again.

 You will never know how desperately I want to say yes, Patrick. Yearning to accept your offer has little to do with the lure of a comfortable existence, but everything to do with the joy of passing the days with you. I will thank you for this gift for the remainder of my life on earth. No matter what else befalls me, this treasure will carry me through on the currents of time.

Your penfriend,
Catherine

Letter from Catherine

155 Hudson Street
New York City
June 2, 1850

Dear Jane,

    I hope you are well in our quiet village and that your house fund is progressing. With you, I do not have to pretend contentment or feign bravery I do not possess. What a relief to remove my facade of efficiency briefly and be myself. You allow no whining, but in making my way, there are steps forward and back. However, I rarely proceed in a straight line. I miss our seaside retreat, as the pace of life here is hectic and jarring. Often, I daydream about our walks to the village and how comforting your wise words have always been to me.

    Tor always warned me, "No good can come from being away from your family." Of course, part of me is tempted to turn tail and run to the comfort of loved ones. I cannot let loneliness increase my fear of being independent while still striving to become a governess, however out of reach. I am alone in a way my family will never know. This freedom I yearn for can sometimes seem like a prison, whittling away at me.

    When I braid my dear Delphina's hair, I think of you. As I lay the long blond plaits one over the other, I sense the power of your words: "We will weave a story into our lives of how our spirits connect in harmony." More than the prayers I was taught as a child, this soothes me. Thank you for your wisdom, Jane, and for the sound of your voice in the night easing my fears.

Your friend,
Catherine

Letter from Jane

Division Street
Sag Harbor, New York
July 2, 1850

Dear Catherine,

    I liked what you said about braiding. The spirits are present, and you will be whole again soon. Life is lonely here on Division Street without you. You are lucky that you live in such a fine house and can use your gifts. That is what they are, Catherine. Learning so much and being able to teach it to others is a source of light. The spirits have sent you there for that important reason. You must try to learn what else they are planning.

    Spending time at my church keeps me well. I have friends and family there who care about me. It helps me bide my time through these quieter days here. As before, I always save a share of my wages for my future house. I can be patient if I need to because I have many plans. Keep braiding, Catherine.

Your friend,
Jane

Letter from Johnny

Tomasina Farm
Scuttle Hole Road
Bridgehampton, New York
July 7, 1850

Dear Cath,

    Thank you for meeting me at the wharf. Seeing your face as soon as I started down the gangway was one of the thrills of my life. I am only sorry that I could not have a longer visit with you. Please forgive my rough written English. It is my duty to improve now that I am in America, and I will no longer write in Gaelic. I have entrusted Frank with correcting my grammar. He is giving me lessons in writing English so I can improve quickly. I was never the student my younger "brother"

Cousin Jack, who taught himself English, became. He dreams of attending medical school and becoming a doctor. That is not my choice, but with his determination, we will call him Doctor Jack someday.

It is hard to accept that I have lost you again after being separated so young. I was only twelve when the three of you left. The years took away more than our parents, my late childhood, and my family's separation from me. I loathe admitting that I am having difficulty adjusting to Sag Harbor. Everyone tries to comfort me because I lived through the famine, which changed me, and not for the better. I am glad that Mam and Da never had to see it. If only I had heeded my family's urging to leave sooner.

I still have bad dreams where I am sent to the Carrickmacross Workhouse. Over one thousand people died there during the famine. The Fever Hospital also saw hundreds perish. Enduring those times was a tall price to pay for an education, but I would not have received it here. I am fortunate to be steeped in the classics, which will enrich me for life. However, if my lessons had been in English, I, too, might be employable as a teacher. Before I left, I opened a bank account for Jack's medical education with the funds you sent. It helped ease my parting, and our uncle and cousin seemed especially pleased that you promised to send more.

My life seems paused. Susie has been so kind to me, and secretly, I sometimes pretend she is you. The curious thing is that I think she knows and tries even more to imitate you. Even a substitute big sister is better than none, although no one can take your place in my heart. Having Frank back as my big brother is my genuine hope for regaining my footing. He remains my best friend and champion. My circumstances enabled me to rise above a terrible situation in Ireland, and I will always be grateful for that.

Your younger brother,
Johnny

Letter from Catherine

155 Hudson Street
New York City
August 1, 1850

Dear Johnny,

Welcome home for the first time, Johnny. Seeing you at the wharf restored my heart. Despite all your challenges, you have grown into a magnificent young man. You will adjust, but under the best circumstances, it takes time. After witnessing so much devastation, please be patient and proceed slowly.

You are in a place where an Irishman has a better chance of an opportunity than in New York City. Just promise me you will not sign up for a whaling voyage. I hope you follow in your oldest brother's footsteps. He is succeeding as a budding American farmer, more so than many immigrants. Most of all, I am relieved you have joined your family on this side of the ocean.

Your loving sister,
Cath

Letter from Susie, in Gaelic

Tomasina Farm
Scuttle Hole Road
Bridgehampton, New York
August 5, 1850

Dear Cath,

I am sorry to say your Johnny is not the boy he was after suffering through the famine years. I know you long to comfort him, but are not free to leave your position. Tor and Frank are ready to bear the duty. Our farm is growing, so it is easier to help Johnny get started. Minnie is big enough to play a bit with Francis, which helps keep them busy. Johnny is already helping with the children, as he is good with them from taking care of Cousin Jack.

Not only Johnny is gaining from Tor's help. We have a steady passage of newcomers from Ireland to Sag Harbor, beyond just family. Saint Andrew's Church is quickly becoming too small. The first thing any new people do is come to see Tor for advice. He always makes the time, even though he has been running the farm with little help because of the gold rush flight. All the new folks are building a community where I hope Johnny will feel at home. Our neighbor, old Mr. Elisha Halsey, paid your brother a memorable compliment: "Tor may not be the first Irishman in the area, but he is generally regarded as the most well-known and respected."

Take care of yourself, dear Cath. I miss you.

Your oldest friend,
Susie

Letter from Catherine

155 Hudson Street
New York City
August 11, 1850

Dear Jane,

My family wants me to visit, but I keep delaying. The real reason I do not want to go home is that there are too many memories. Men are still sending letters home from the gold rush, and that is a subject I want to avoid. My mind has not changed, and I still do not want to hear from Michael. I tell myself, *I stopped loving Michael the day our baby died and never want to see him again.*

Ellen does not speak of her brother, though I noticed letters for her forwarded from Greenport. Whether by mistake or on purpose, Ellen left a letter from Michael on the table outside her room. When I passed her door, walking down the hall from my room, I picked it up. Against my better judgment, I read it. I translated and copied the letter here to ask you if I am, indeed, a bad person.

From Michael

Trinity County, California
March 16, 1850

Dear Ellie,
 The gold rush is about as rewarding as chasing whales, as both are filthy, degenerate, and bankrupt. I am sorry that the description is so harsh. Life here is just that, and there is no way to sweeten it. If I sound bitter, you are right. I find some gold in my pan, but it does not amount to much, with high food and supply prices. So little profit is in the offing that William and I are considering leaving. There is a chance of one more gold strike up in Weaverville before we give up.
 Ellie, I need your help. I still cannot locate my wife, and I urgently need to reach her. It is very discouraging, and I am frightened for her safety. I will leave here tomorrow, but I do not know where to go to find Cathy. Her brother Frank must be here in California because all the letters came back. I will not bother with her brother Tor, who hates me and would return my letter. My old shipmates, who knew her, are all here in California, as are the lads from the shipyard. I cannot remember anyone else to write to. If you think of someone who could help, please write to me.

Your loving brother,
Mike

The pang I felt was much more for Ellen than Michael, but I also felt remorse for him. I callously left Ellen in the position of continually lying to her brother. To you, Jane, I will make one of what you always call my Irish declarations: I have done wrong and resolve to make amends to Ellen for putting her in an untenable situation.
 I also disappoint Ellen by not being the sounding board she needs. I am responsible for her, as it was my idea that she would come, and I made a promise. When I conclude my day teaching the children and she suggests, "Let us walk through Saint John's Park," I shake my head from side to side. Ellen does not know that I am still recovering from grief, as I have not told her. I cannot burden her with more secrets.
 Fortunately, with her warm personality, she has befriended the rest

of the staff, even the chilly tutor, Mr. Fenton. The cook said, "Ellen is a breath of fresh air in this house." The staff's friendliness only goes so far. She wants a suitor, but there is none in the offing.

Ellen goes for walks with Ann, the other young maid, in the house. They are hoping for conversation with the young footmen tending the neighbors' horses and carriages. At the sound of a knock at the kitchen door, both girls call in unison, "I will answer it." They hope that the young man making a delivery might be a suitable beau. I wish I could help, but at least there are more young men in New York than where you are.

As for Michael, yes, my heart of stone managed a spoonful of sympathy. It quickly hardened again when I contemplated he had only himself to blame. I turn to you again for more guidance and sincerely hope that I am not exhausting you with my problems. I shudder to think of my life without the outlet of writing to you, Jane.

Your friend,
Catherine

Letter from Jane

Division Street
Sag Harbor, New York
September 14, 1850

Dear Catherine,

You are not a bad person, but with all that talking, you can be a trying one. The way you circle around and around a problem can trap you inside. I am glad that my example means something to you. The beliefs I was taught have helped me and, in turn, you. Still they can be very different from what you were taught coming up.

My people see women in a different way from yours. Only since the English came did our people see men try to control women. In the Algonquin ways, we women have never been less than men. There are even stories that still survive that we were once above men. In our traditions, a wife may leave a husband. There is no shame, and a woman can decide for herself. Our tradition of laboring beside each other made women's voices heard, and our ideas were put to use. We have been members of the tribal councils and made decisions with the men.

Because of this, we see ourselves as different from you women from Europe. There is a feeling of calm, knowing we do not have to fight to be seen. Our necks are longer because we do not have to nod when we do not agree. Backs are straighter because we do not bow to men. Voices are clear because we do not have to raise them to be heard. We move easier with our simpler clothing and trappings. Seeing ourselves through the eyes of friends brings peace.

You have made your choices, so now they belong to you. Go forward bravely. Looking to the side twists your path forward, and turning your head around will bring you to a halt. Walk tall and proud ahead.

Your friend,
Jane

Letter from Frank

Division Street
Sag Harbor, New York
October 30, 1850

Dear Cath,

It has been just over a year since Johnny came to Bridgehampton. Just as he was adjusting to life over here, he became the next victim infected with gold rush fever. I told him, "Johnny, how can you think about leaving when you just got here? Give things a chance to improve before you abscond to more parts unknown." Arguing with a young man is futile. Almost everyone within ten years of his age from the area has already gone. So instead of trying to stop Johnny, Cath, my girl, I am joining him.

I can see that little foot of yours stamping already. Wharf labor has shrunk to almost nothing. Going after gold is the only way I can feed my family. Some fellows off recently returned ships have said California is a disappointment, but the situation here is beyond that. A guarantee of less gold is better than a guarantee of no employment.

Save your strength in putting pen to paper arguing, Cath, my girl, because we have already booked our passages through New York. At least we will see you before we sail. Though it has been going on for a few years, the gold rush is still far from over. Apparently, more stream beds are still to be discovered in the more remote hills of California. We have nothing to lose by going. Please understand that your brothers must give this a chance.

Yours forever,
Frank

Letter from Catherine, in Gaelic

155 Hudson Street
New York City
January 9, 1851

Dear Susie,

How unfair to you and Tor that Isabella and Mamie are your responsibility now. The boys' reasoning for going to the gold rush remains flawed, as most local men have made the same argument. There is neither the energy nor the will to combat it. Only your husband, this family's stalwart patriarch, seems to be exempt from the mania. I witnessed the biblical exodus of our villages directly. The fever's power, once the infection takes hold, is almost impossible to break. I gave up trying a long time ago and bade farewell to the boys at the wharf.

It was thrilling seeing Johnny, a fully mature man. He has become even more handsome and strong since arriving here. I had forgotten how much I loved his dreamy eyes. I apologized for not coming home, but did not tell him why. It was to avoid being confronted about Michael by any number of people. "So sorry that my employers would not allow it," was my meager response to Johnny. Call me a coward, Susie.

Having to turn around and say goodbye to my younger brother once again was heart-wrenching. I regret not having the nerve to confront my actions when I owed Johnny more of a welcome here. Add it to the list of my accumulating selfish acts. At least Frank will be with him as a protective big brother. His parting words, shouted to me from the deck, were, "If I see Michael, I will tell him you say hello." I have lived so many lives since landing on that same wharf ten years before that anything is possible.

Your oldest friend,
Cath

Space and Time! now I see it is true, what I guess'd at,
What I guess'd when I loaf'd on the grass,
What I guess'd while I lay alone in my bed,
And again as I walk'd the beach under the paling stars of the morning.

"Song of Myself," 33
Leaves of Grass
Walt Whitman

Chapter Five

1852–1857

Letter from Catherine

155 Hudson Street
New York City
December 9, 1852

Dear Mr. Melville,

Perhaps you remember me. I served you in the tavern of the Nassau Hotel in Sag Harbor, right before *Typee* was published. Your recent novel, *Moby-Dick; or, The Whale*, is a revelation. I found it profoundly stirring, exciting, and thrilling. It also chilled me with the stark reality of danger on the high seas. Maybe it affected me so much because I married a whaleman soon after I met you. Now I see the dark secret you so eloquently laid bare within each seaman's soul. They wish to tempt death and come back alive to tell the tale.

You seem to say that whaling is a kind of madness. Those who succumb to its call are possessed. You expose and confirm my fear that whaling is a destination of darkness, one with no sure route of return. Please correct me if I am interpreting the text wrong.

Thank you for making plain what others either deny or only hint at. Knowing I did not imagine my worst fears helps in some torturous way. One doubts oneself when people brush such concerns aside. Presenting the truth within our souls through your artistry will make an impact that will long be remembered. Thank you for what you have given us.

Your devoted reader,
Catherine M. Heffernan

~

Letter from Herman Melville

Pittsfield, Massachusetts
March 8, 1853

Dear Mrs. Heffernan,
 There was a young woman I vaguely remember speaking with at the Nassau Hotel. I recall your straightforward and opinionated ways, all offered in a spirited brogue while pouring rum. My sincere condolences that you married a whaleman. Becoming a whaling widow is a fate I would not have wished for an educated young woman. Other proper young ladies who should know better have also met your fate.
 It must be difficult to imagine your husband navigating the dangers in the book. In his defense, they were dramatized to create reader interest, though you may overlook that explanation. Take heart, Mrs. Heffernan. Perhaps your husband will come home and stay. I am proof it sometimes happens.
 Thank you for your compliments about the book, but I wish the critics were as kind. I also thank you for buying it, as the sales are disappointing. As for my intentions, I am tasked with offering a gesture but have no dominion over its reception.

Yours truly,
Herman Melville

~

Letter from Catherine, in Gaelic

155 Hudson Street
New York City
September 8, 1853

Dear Susie,

When I was running an errand for Mrs. Bechet on Worth Street, I found myself engaged in a likely historic battle. As I approached the corner church, a raucous crowd spilled out. People shouted and jeered at each other, though it appeared to be mostly men shouting at women. Though there were plenty of women shouting back.

All my instincts were to run for safety, but something propelled me through the crowd into the Broadway Tabernacle. On the lectern was a woman in a skirt well above her ankles, with baggy pantalettes showing underneath. She read from a written statement, "Woman must be recognized politically, legally, socially, and religiously the equal of man." I picked up a program and saw that her name was Lucy Stone. A man shouted, "Take off your bloomers!" I guessed that is what they called her strange leg coverings. The program said she was a graduate of Oberlin College, one of the few colleges in the United States to admit women. I was not aware that any women went to college.

The following speaker was even more surprising. Her name was Sojourner Truth. The ruffians calling from the balcony had to be restrained by the police as she tried to address the assembly. She stood ramrod straight and tall and said calmly, "I am a citizen of the State of New York; I was born in it, and I was a slave in the State of New York; and now I am a good citizen of the State of New York." She compared the hissing and booing of the men present to "the spirit of a goose and the spirit of a snake." The next day, the newspaper dubbed it the "mob convention" because of all the men jeering and carrying on.

After a few days, I recovered from the shock of the meeting. I was so curious that I went to the library and read about the Women's Rights Convention held in Seneca Falls. It was surprising enough to listen to women speak about our rights from a podium. In upstate New York, they went further and wrote a document. It resembled the Founding Fathers' Declaration of Independence, called the Declaration of Sentiments.

It was startling to read because while the ideas had never been expressed before, they resonated with me. We should be able to inherit property from our families, sign a contract, or keep our children in a separation. Still I cannot imagine a world where we could.

Jane Perdue told me that in her people's traditions, women always had these rights. Perhaps that is what Mrs. Cady Stanton meant when she wrote in the declaration, "Let us imagine more than what we see in front of us, which may exist elsewhere."

The last proposal in the Declaration of Sentiments is the most challenging to imagine: "Women should have the right to vote." I had not previously considered the idea, but it also resounds once the boldness lessens. We pay taxes, like the members of the Boston Tea Party who rebelled when they had no representation, as we do not. There is much food for thought about what the future holds for generations to come. As the mother of little Minnie, think about warning her when she is older. American women may be different when she grows up.

Your oldest friend,
Cath

Letter from Susie, in Gaelic

Tomasina Farm
Scuttle Hole Road
Bridgehampton, New York
October 8, 1853

Dear Cath,

The gathering sounds more like a pub brawl back home than a meeting in a church. I have never heard of the Seneca Falls convention, as I barely have time to look at the *Sag Harbor Corrector*. Since baby Edward arrived, if I take my eyes off the three little ones for one moment, something bad happens. Usually, I have spittle and sour milk all down the front of my apron.

Beyond the fence and the horizon, it could be a changing time, but I would be the last to find out. We left the Old World behind across the sea and with it, the old ways. As far as I can tell, farm life is pretty much the same here.

You sound more like the hearty girl I used to know. Mrs. Cady Stanton wrote something different from any woman I have ever heard.

Even when my written English is better, I cannot imagine ever voting in an election. They would be vexed by me carting three children to vote. To think my little Minnie could grow up and do such a thing. I would stay home with her children so she could be free to cast her vote.

Your oldest friend,
Susie

Letter from Catherine

155 Hudson Street
New York City
October 12, 1853

Dear Patrick,

 I hope you are well. I wanted to reassure you that I have fared better since our last exchange. Your caring words carry me through life's challenges daily. It also helps to have a refuge outside the Bechet house. Mine is Saint Peter's Church, a short walk away on Barclay Street. No one there questions my presence, complains about my accent, or notices my lack of depositing alms in the wooden box. The library is another retreat, but several blocks farther. Only on Saturdays, when our class is not in session, can I take advantage of its wonders.

 I sometimes slip inside Saint Peter's on early morning errands. The still, darkened interior gives me a feeling of peace, and I can escape the city's tumult and life itself. Several times, an elegant, very elderly gentleman said, "Please come sit with me." "Not today, sir," I always replied. My parents taught me not to befriend strange men. However, one day, my desperation for someone to talk to besides Ellen emboldened me to ask, "Is this seat taken?" His kind smile beckoned.

 "My name is Pierre Toussaint, and I am a retired hairdresser." He was also something of a legend, I would later learn. However, in these stolen moments in my prescribed life, he was a refuge. I enjoyed walking him home, as he was unsteady on his feet. It gave us the ideal time to confide in one another. What a delight to have a friend I can talk to about books and subjects like history and philosophy, all in French. Spending time with Pierre made me remember the contented woman I used to be. He took my arm and trained his attention on me, making me feel like the world's most important person.

An usher at the church confided in me, "Mr. Toussaint was one of the founders of the first Catholic school for Black children and opened his home to orphans for years." One day, Pierre asked me to take a walk with him. We approached Saint Patrick's Cathedral graveyard on Mulberry Street, where he led me to a grave. "This is where our adopted daughter, Euphemia, is buried. She died of consumption at fourteen years old. Her mother, my beloved sister Rosalie, died of it as well when Euphemia was a baby. It is such a terrible disease. Someday, I will be buried here with them." It seems I am imparting another sad story, but spoken by Pierre, it sounded hopeful. Having you as a penfriend has been a godsend, Patrick. Now I am delighted to also have a friend in person.

Your penfriend,
Catherine

*

Letter from Pierre Toussaint, in French

144 Franklin Street
New York City
October 19, 1853

Dear Catherine,

You have asked for my life story. Writing is easier than speaking while walking on tired legs. We are already truants whispering in the back of the church like naughty children, so paper is safer. I was born into slavery in Saint Domingue in 1766. I took my last name in honor of an ex-slave, General Toussaint L'Ouverture. He was the leader of a slave rebellion that won their freedom and forged Saint Domingue into the country of Haiti.

I came to New York with the wealthy plantation owner Pierre Berard in 1787. The family owned my great-grandmother, who was captured in Africa. Her daughter, my grandmother, was taught to read and write. She, in turn, taught me. Although I remained a slave, Mrs. Berard allowed me to apprentice as a hairdresser. Soon I was earning good wages, as the older wealthy ladies were fond of me. My tips were generous and plentiful. I have even tended the hair of your employer's mother-in-law, Mrs. Chardon.

Years later, Mrs. Berard became a widow and lost all her money. I cared for her, and she freed me in her will when I was forty-one. With my income, I purchased the freedom of my wife, Juliette, and our adopted daughter. You could say it became my pastime to purchase other slaves' freedom with my gratuities from wealthy ladies.

Saint Peter's is my other home, and I come almost daily. Like you, I like to sit and enjoy the peace. I will save a seat for you in our usual spot at the back of the church. Look for me in the pew I let below the painting of my friend Elizabeth Seton. Consider reflecting on our last conversation about not waiting for mercy, but practicing it.

Your friend,
Pierre

Letter from Catherine, in French

155 Hudson Street
New York City
October 30, 1853

Dear Pierre,

Thank you for sharing your story with me. You have lived an extraordinary life. That you take the time to be interested in me is a welcome surprise. I have pondered long and hard about your teachings on mercy. Such a simple word can have so many meanings. It can mean forgiveness, kindness, compassion, sympathy, leniency, and many more. I am not sure where to begin, although I fear I am deficient in each meaning. Can you tell me which is the most important?

Mercy can also mean grace. When I am with you, life becomes elevated, imbued with meaning. No one I have ever met has had that effect on me. Your friendship has renewed me and restored my hope for the future. Before you came into my life, my point of view was bleak, and I could not find my way ahead. I look forward to many days of friendship and fellowship with you.

Your friend,
Catherine

Letter from Pierre Toussaint, in French

144 Franklin Street
New York City
February 1, 1853

Dear Catherine,

Mercy is an elusive collaborator. I have often called on it when the ladies complained about my hairdressing. It is precisely then that one could change perspective and question what is occurring in the heart of the disappointed lady. To express dissatisfaction is to feel something is lacking. That lack may be a good feeling about oneself. These ladies have graced me with their presence so I can make them feel better. Just because they are rich and privileged does not mean they do not have hearts and cannot feel pain.

When I have done my best to make them beautiful, and they do not behold it, I must help them see. First, I ask them, "When were you happiest?" Often, they say, "It was when I was a child receiving a gift for my birthday." Then I ask them, "When were you saddest?" Frequently, I have heard, "My father scolded me for being naughty." I tell them, "How wonderful it is that you are no longer a child but a beautiful woman."

They sit up and begin to relax. I tell them my thoughts as I dress their hair: "If I get this curl to bend and this sweep of hair to stay, I will have transformed Madame into a beautiful swan." As the lady inspects herself in the mirror, her doubts recede. A smile spreads as she pats her hair and turns from side to side. I have accomplished my mission of elevating the spirit of each woman in our special time together.

You see, it is not the woman speaking when the complaints come. It is the little girl who has been harshly judged. I want to soothe and comfort her when her papa criticizes her or clap my hands in unison for a lovely birthday gift. I see that little girl inside the grown woman, and I love her. What an honor to be able to give such a small but tender gesture each day.

Now, my ladies have left this earth, as I soon will, but I am still blessed. It is also an honor to see my lovely young friend with that distant look in her eyes, as though she were gazing out at the infinite sea. Who is it that you see on the horizon?

Love,
Pierre

Letter from Catherine

155 Hudson Street
New York City
November 5, 1853

Dear Patrick,

Once again, I hope you can tolerate more, as my litany of sad news continues unabated. One recent morning, I stopped by Saint Peter's only to be told that Pierre Toussaint had passed away at the age of eighty-seven. My abiding friendship has ended, and I will cease to bask in his wisdom, advice, and caring. I will always remember his presence at the church, which will continue to be my refuge whenever I have a moment.

Pierre was buried next to his beloved daughter. Ironically, my friend's name was translated from French as "all saints" because he was actually one dwelling on this earth. Yet even he had difficulty instilling mercy in this mere mortal's soul. I am sorry that you never met him. Your caring carries me through this loss.

Your friend,
Catherine

Letter from Patrick

653 Water Street
New York City
November 17, 1853

Dear Catherine,

Please accept my condolences on the loss of your friend. I am alternately happy and frustrated to be near you again in New York. Our peripatetic courting has been relegated back to the page. Visiting each other remains ill-advised for the sake of propriety.

While I still feel sad that my proposal was rebuffed, I was certainly not surprised. I understand that the scheme of running away together was daring and illicit. However, many people start over in these unprecedented times. That is precisely what I have done since coming back to New York.

Please understand how difficult this news is for me to deliver. Despite my joy, I fear it will close a door between us for good. I have met a lovely young lady named Julia. She came here with her family from Cork, and my colleague, her brother, introduced us. We are to be married soon and will spend our honeymoon in Nicaragua. Her willingness to go there surprised me, but Julia loves to travel. She is eight years younger than I am and has more energy.

I took a suite of rooms in a building on Water Street for our return. I continue to marvel that, after so long alone, I have finally found a lovely woman to become my wife. This will also be my first proper home on American soil.

Despite my happiness, part of me will never be complete. There will always be space in my heart for what might have been. Still I must look forward. As I once told you, "I accept what I can obtain instead of yearning for what is out of reach."

Your penfriend,
Patrick

Letter from Catherine

155 Hudson Street
New York City
November 30, 1853

Dear Patrick,

How happy I am for you. I am not surprised you were not to remain a bachelor. With your handsome face, manners, and business acumen, you are one of the more eligible young men in New York. I would have joined your long line of admirers if I were not a married woman.

I am glad the lovely Julia is the winner of your affections. She is lucky to have you, which I am sure she knows. What an admirable trait she enjoys voyages, and how impressive you can enjoy it together. I can attest that some men would refuse their wives as traveling companions, especially on long voyages. Perhaps I will sit with Julia and discuss how cavalier a single young girl once was. Who would pass on such an opportunity to marry you? On second thought, the subject is probably best left in the past.

Now that you are to be settled, Patrick, I want to assure you that your previous worries on my behalf are unfounded. Yes, I have lost my dear friend Pierre. Fortunately, his example has renewed my appreciation of my sister-in-law Ellen as a companion. While at first, she was an added and weighty responsibility, lately our roles have changed. Though I have not always treated her as she deserves, Ellen has become a comfort and solace for me.

Everyone else has remained at a distance except for her. I take her for granted, but Ellen is my best friend. She keeps me company, makes me laugh, and cares for me. I am indeed lucky to have such a sister. I have long ago ceased to regard her as just a sister-in-law.

Never have I regretted the limitation of our friendship existing only on paper as much as now. How joyous it would be to see you walk down the aisle with your blushing bride, but how could we explain to the wedding guests and family why an old shipmate of the opposite sex was attending?

Our companionship must stay relegated to vellum unless it has served its purpose. Much of our correspondence has been predicated on loneliness, but that does not apply anymore. I would understand if you wanted to spend your time enjoying your young bride instead of an old acquaintance.

Your penfriend,
Catherine

Letter from Patrick

653 Water Street
New York City
December 18, 1853

Dear Catherine,

I am pleased that your sister-in-law is such a fine companion. It warms my soul to know you are not alone. Sometimes, the answer to our dilemmas is right in front of us.

As for your suggestion to cease penfriendship, please do not doubt me. Nothing could deter me from pursuing our correspondence. It has sustained me over these years in a way you will never know. Admittedly, sometimes it frustrated me that our friendship could not progress to something more. It was not for lack of trying on my part.

When I was at my lowest, I always had the promise of an expected letter from you to cheer me on. I cannot turn my back on our friendship because I have become a married man. What we have has always been ours alone, and always will be. Please promise to continue to be my penfriend, Catherine.

Your penfriend,
Patrick

Letter from Catherine

155 Hudson Street
New York City
January 9, 1854

Dear Patrick,
  How could I ever doubt your kindness and loyalty? Perhaps I overreacted at the thought of coming between you and your new wife. This is neither the time nor the place to admit what I must say. Since you alluded to the same emotion, I will proceed. Along the way, I, too, have regretted what might have been, perhaps even bitterly.
  Please forgive my indulgence, as it serves no useful purpose now. That I prophesied my bitter reaction does not excuse it. Yet your honesty took me aback and emboldened a retort that shall never be revisited. You have taught me to look forward, and I have no regrets. Teaching is still my occupation and joy. I still consider it a mission that fills me with pride and gratitude.
  From now on, I look forward to hearing any news about your new family. I am sure more joy is coming your way. Julia is most fortunate to have a husband like you. Wishing you many years of wedded bliss.

Your penfriend,
Catherine

Letter from Susie, in Gaelic

Tomasina Farm
Scuttle Hole Road
Bridgehampton, New York
February 9, 1854

Dear Cath,
  I am with child once again, and I am happy. I do admit to you, and only you, that I am also wondering how I will manage my newest blessing. The gift of four children will surely be a test. While still a bit peevish, Francis, almost seven years old, is good with his hands. He boasts, "I can already hammer nails, whittle toys, and fix broken things for my ma

in the house." Soon I will lose him to farm chores, as he is already feeding the chickens. My loss will be Tor's gain.

We are between farmhands, as Isabella's brother and the others we hired went to the gold rush. Tor will have four extra hands one day when all the children grow up. When Minnie is older, I will rely on her help with the new baby. Even now, she can get little Edward to play with her before they fight over a toy. She loves her baby clothespin doll with flax for hair.

I enjoy gossiping about your much more exciting life and depend on it. Without your letters to look forward to, I would become gloomy. They are needed to break up the day-to-day routine of farm life. If I could be someone else for a day, I would choose you. I am curious to see what being on my own is like. You might also enjoy trading lives with me for a day. Writing to you gets me out of my rut and helps me think of new things, which is good. Take care of yourself, dear Cath.

Your oldest friend,
Susie

Letter from Susie, in Gaelic

Tomasina Farm
Scuttle Hole Road
Bridgehampton, New York
March 11, 1854

Dear Cath,

My life has taken a terrible turn. I lost the baby. Little Arthur was born and died within a few days. Now I see what you went through. I am not as weak or sick as you were, which may be the only reason I have kept going. I do not have a choice. Every part of me wants to stop and lie down. But the children need their meals, and the animals must be fed.

I am walking through the days as a creature of the night. With no sleep, I do not know how I keep going. The children grab my legs and call up to me, trying to get me to answer them. I try to nod and pat them, so they are not afraid. They know something terrible happened but cannot guess what it is.

I am afraid that the emptiness will not stop. I want to be myself again. It feels like I am breaking into little pieces. Francis stays with me and holds my hand. He does some of my chores, so Tor will not know. Even Minnie tries to brush my hair. Little Edward just cries and cries. I carry him around and around the table, and we cry together. Come to me, Cath.

Your oldest friend,
Susie

Letter from Catherine, in Gaelic

155 Hudson Street
New York City
April 3, 1854

Dear Susie,

I hope the worst has passed. When I left, I saw a glimmer of a smile on your face, which gave me hope. Even under the worst circumstances, being with you again filled my heart with joy. Bearing grief with you gave me a depth of feeling I had forgotten about. You are my true sister, the only one I will ever have. I am sorry you had to join the other sisterhood we share, grievers of lost children.

I believe you will heal and recover. Certain platitudes are spouted during these times, but they are for a reason. You need to hear, "You must go on for your children who need you. You must stay strong for them. Your husband needs you and would be lost without you." Susie, there is so much in your life, and you will find your way through this darkness. You are strong in body and mind, and that will help you. Take one slow step at a time.

During my time, my friend Jane told me to listen to the spirits. She said, "Let the spirits speak to you now in your dreams, and they will save you." It happened, Susie, just like she said. Listen and a path will open. I am praying for you, dear friend. You are never alone because you have me.

Your oldest friend,
Cath

Letter from Susie, in Gaelic

Tomasina Farm
Scuttle Hole Road
Bridgehampton, New York
May 22, 1854

Dear Cath,
    When you took my hand, you caught me when I was falling fast. Only you beside me and your hand squeezing mine could have stopped it. Thank you, Cath, for everything: the children, the cooking, the chores, and the washing. I do not know what I would have done without you there next to me. So far, I have not heard any spirits, but we did get a new litter of puppies. The children are overjoyed with them, running around the yard. They are so lovable that I even let one in the house, but the rest stayed in the barn.
    You did come to take my place, just as I put forth in my last letter. Even though I will not be able to do the same in your life, I am still glad you got a bit of mine. It makes me feel even more like a sister to you. I am beginning to pretend again, so that is a good sign. I did what you said and braided Minnie's hair. To my surprise, it did help, with a peaceful feeling inside me while I held her little locks. When things become hard again, I will make believe I am walking in St. John Park arm in arm with you, gossiping together. It has been my holiday before, and it will again.

Your oldest friend,
Susie

Letter from Jane

Division Street
Sag Harbor, New York
September 19, 1854

Dear Catherine,

I once told you, "You will not have to look far for people in need, as they will be sent to you." That is indeed what has happened, as now it is your turn to help heal.

You were surprised by the change in Sag Harbor during your brief visit with me away from Susie. When the men were away on the whaleships, they were always coming and going. With the gold rush, most of the men are gone at the same time and all together. As the village continues to empty, so do the businesses. Many stores now have For Rent signs in the windows. People have lost their labor, but I am not complaining. My employer has money, and my position will continue.

After my past ill will toward Mr. Mulford, I am thankful for steady labor in these hard times. I have tried to lead by example by turning the other cheek, which may have done some good with him. He has become more patient toward me and acts kinder. Maybe he even misses our busy port. This small turn in my fortunes is good enough for me.

Thank you for the gift of *Moby-Dick; or, The Whale* for my collection. I look forward to reading it to learn what my husband, brother-in-law, cousins, and uncles have done as whalemen. A few years ago, Silas's cousin Jason, who was only twenty-two years old, was lost at sea. I have spent so much time imagining life aboard a whaling vessel, and now I will know.

I also bought *Narrative of the Life of Frederick Douglass, an American Slave*. My china collection is coming along slowly. Someday, when I have my house, there will be a whole set to show on a shelf in my parlor. You will be my guest, and we will have tea.

Your friend,
Jane

SUSAN MCGUIRK

Letter from Catherine

155 Hudson Street
New York City
October 21, 1854

Dear Jane,

    You were right. I did not need to look far for anyone to help. Seeing Susie under the veil of sorrow broke my heart. Finding a woman I have always known and loved stricken with grief was terrible to endure. I felt unprepared to rescue her despite having been in the same situation. It brought the pain back to me, but this time was different. I tried to imitate you as I strived to offer her a path out of the darkness. Only your words penetrated my ears: "The spirits led us to each other to help heal the pain of our lost ones."

    I had to stay next to Susie because only a fellow wounded mother would be accepted. Even saying nothing was far better than not being there. It took several days of handholding, soothing, lulling, and murmuring for Susie to come out of her state of shock. She began to hear and respond better. Slight movements defined her return to the present. She arranged the covers on the bed and fussed with her hair.

    I did as many chores as I could and fed the children. In her last letter, Susie jokingly suggested that we take each other's places in our lives, and I never believed it would come true. Being a mother of three children was astonishing, if only briefly. I have rarely labored so hard in my life. When I compared toiling at the hotels or on the farm in Mullinclavin, Susie's tasks were more taxing.

    I left with a newfound appreciation of my livelihood and relief that I had my quiet room to return to. However, it also made me realize Susie had always been right. As she said in a letter, "We would be lost in each other's lives, as we were always different."

    As the days passed, Susie came back bit by bit. Tor was a tremendous help with the children, which allowed for the requisite time with Susie. She rallied for them when they came and sat on the bed with her. That is when I knew she would recover.

    It was a reprieve to come home and have time to ponder the meaning of the loss. While I still consider myself the mother of a departed one, my life as a teacher was possible because of it. Nonetheless I would trade my employment for another chance at motherhood in a moment. No matter how much I love teaching and look forward to resuming, it does not replace what was lost.

Life is an enigma. We must lose to gain, like sowing and reaping. I lost one profession and gained another. Susie lost her child, but she is still a young woman. You have become a helpmeet through your trials, which I, and many others, continue to benefit from. Happy reading, Jane.

Your friend,
Catherine

Letter from Catherine

155 Hudson Street
New York City
June 1, 1855

Dear Tor,

When I received word that Johnny and Frank were coming home, I knew the exodus to California was finally over. With heavy hearts and dimmed expectations, our brothers booked their passage back to New York. When I met them at the wharf, I barely recognized the two disheveled strangers with long beards and grimy clothes.

It took Frank shouting, "Cath, my girl!" for me to pick out our brother from the crowd. The boys had both aged, and the light in their eyes had faded. It was not until the familiar bear hugs enveloped me that I believed they were our Frank and Johnny.

Like many thousands of others, their pans held multitudes of sand but barely a nugget of gold. Unlike the wreckage of the abandoned whaleships from Sag Harbor left in the harbor of San Francisco, our brothers at least came home.

The boys got on the steamship to Sag Harbor to mend what was left of their scattered lives. They will arrive in port possessing much less than before they left. Their families have fared no better. Your wisdom stood alone in resisting the fever. Thank you for giving us someone to count on these past years, Tor.

Your loving sister,
Cath

❦

Letter from Frank

Rose Farm
Hayground
Bridgehampton, New York
October 7, 1855

Dear Cath,
 My life was going in the right direction after the gold rush calamity. My shipbuilding occupation in Brookhaven seemed like a dream come true. Even though it forced me to live away from my family, I was grateful to secure labor. After the debt I incurred from the gold rush, my wages were enough to begin again. I enjoyed shipbuilding and liked my mates there. It was difficult riding the half-day journey each week, instead of every day, to see my girls, but I was earning ample wages.
 I felt devastated when it all disappeared, enduring another setback. In one big circle, I am now living the life of a farmhand, back where I started as a lad. I should be thankful for having any labor, but after stretching our pathetic little plot in Ireland for so long, I cannot help my distaste. It clashes with my nature to only have a donkey to talk to.
 On a happier note, you are now hearing from a citizen of the United States. Before the shipyard closed, my managers there sponsored me. I am so pleased to be a naturalized American citizen. Chills ran through me when I signed the document, renouncing our English oppressors to embrace our true home.
 Thankfully, Johnny is watching after my girl Mamie, as they are staying on adjacent farms. Being a mile away from her feels like a hundred, but I did not want to upend her young life again now that she is happy where she is. Isabella still will not come home from the

almshouse and is less and less herself when I visit. The ladies there say, "We have seen people lose their memory before, and we recommend letting them be."

I have difficulty accepting their recommendation and allowing my beautiful wife to stay in such a place. What a bitter pill that she lives among paupers and the sick, infirm, and elderly. Please pray she will see reason and agree to leave that miserable place. How cruel life can sometimes be. I would like you to show a little of the mercy you speak of and write to your husband. One lesson I have learned through the continuing trial of the last few years is that we all make mistakes.

Yours forever,
Frank

Letter from Catherine

155 Hudson Street
New York City
November 29, 1855

Dear Frank,

I am sorry about how ill Isabella has become. The poor woman lacks the turtle shell the rest of us pull along for protection. You have tried your best to protect your family, but her illness is not your fault. She can decide her future, and you cannot force her to come home when she refuses. Keep trying, Frank. That is all you can do.

I always considered you a man who understood women better than your brethren, as you always had insight into me. I doubt any man could unlock the mystery of your wife. Now that you have the quiet life of a man of the soil, you may have time to unravel your dilemmas. You have had more than your share of excitement these past few years. I am glad and relieved that Mamie is thriving. As a new farmer, you planted a seed in my mind. You wrote, "Show some of that mercy you talk about and write to your husband." It may please you to know that the seed is taking root.

Yours forever,
Cath

SUSAN MCGUIRK

Letter from Catherine

155 Hudson Street
New York City
December 4, 1855

Dear Mr. Whitman,

 I hope you remember me. When I saw the advertisement in the newspaper, I immediately bought your book of poems, *Leaves of Grass.* You told me you started writing it back in 1848 when we met at the Wyandanch Hotel in Greenport. I loved your book, and it means so much to me. I was surprised to see the words that changed my life not in a poem, but in the preface. "Manhattan's streets I saunter'd pondering." You spoke them aloud to me when I met you. Those words are why I left Long Island.

 I have never tasted or smelled words, beheld their images, or heard their voices before I read *Leaves of Grass.* The natural world you described caused me to shiver and wipe the sea spray from my brow. Words do as you command. You use them to encompass all of creation, and no person or place is excluded. All are present.

 My perception has changed since I read it. I am wider, broader, taller, and farther away simultaneously. My mind is stretched, poked, forced out of corners, and pushed beyond comfort. The world I was born into and thought I knew is forever altered.

 I have also done what you long ago told me: "Move to Manhattan. You belong there." You were right to encourage me to come. I also found my current position through an advertisement in the newspaper. I hope you sell many books from the one you placed.

Your old friend,
Catherine Heffernan

Letter from Walt Whitman

Ryerson Street
Brooklyn, New York

March 3, 1856

Dear Mrs. Heffernan,

Yes, I remember you. Thank you for the compliments on my book, and I am pleased that your move to New York has been successful. I typeset and printed the book myself, but a new edition by a publisher, Fowler and Wells, will be available soon. There are twenty new poems in it, with titles for all of them. The first one, my favorite, is called "Song of Myself."

The line that meant so much to you, "Manhattan's streets I saunter'd pondering," is no longer a mere phrase, as in the preface of the first *Leaves of Grass*. Now it is included in a poem in the new edition titled "Song of Prudence." The poem refers to the notion that anything one does reverberates throughout life. The verse says, "the prudence that suits immortality." I think you will like it.

Your friend,
Walt Whitman

Letter from Patrick

653 Water Street
New York City
April 26, 1856

Dear Catherine,

My joy is beyond measure to announce the birth of our beloved son Michael, nicknamed Mickey. He is my heart, and words cannot describe my joy when I stare into his little face. His mother is also doing well, and both are ably looked after by our housekeeper, Curran.

If someone had told me back in Ireland that this is the life I would live, I would have laughed. In my mind, I am still a portly head boy in hedge school with no friends. I thought I could accept what came my way, but this is more than I ever dreamed of. I fear waking up and finding it has all been taken away. Still, when I look at Mickey, my heart fills with rapture. Forgive me for waxing on. I just cannot believe that a miracle of this magnitude has happened to me.

Your penfriend,
Patrick

༄

Letter from Catherine

155 Hudson Street
New York City
May 9, 1856

Dear Patrick,

What wonderful news! How happy I am that you are a father to little Mickey. I wish you and your son a long and happy life together. Thank you for sharing your joy. You have come so far from the boy I met on the *Queen Victoria*. Congratulations to you and your wife, my friend.

Your struggle to accept all your good fortune may be understandable but unwarranted. If any of us are truly worthy of happiness, it is you, Patrick. As the most decent man I know, you deserve to be a happy father and husband.

For a moment today, I, too, was a mother. Before you drop your spectacles, let me explain. I was walking with my young charge, Delphina Bechet, eight years old, in Saint John's Park. A well-dressed woman approached us and said, "My compliments to your pretty daughter. She looks just like you." Before I could interrupt to correct her, the woman walked briskly by.

Delphina laughed and said, "My dearest wish just came true, Madame. You are my proper mother."

"Delphina," I said, "that is not humorous and is disrespectful to your mama."

"I do not care," she replied. "I love you more than anyone in the world, and I do not care who knows it."

Instead of reprimanding her further, as propriety dictated, I gathered her in a close embrace. I told her, "I love you just as much."

Maybe it was wrong, but I told myself something. *This is my life, and rather than feeling guilty, I will be grateful for the gift of my pretend daughter. She is so much better than not having any. I am fortunate and will continue to be.* However, lying in bed later that night, it would be a lie to say I did not have a pang in my heart. You will be a wonderful father, Patrick.

Your penfriend,
Catherine

Letter from the proprietor of the Wyandanch Hotel

Third Street
Greenport, New York
November 6, 1856

Dear Mrs. Heffernan,

I hope you remember me. You were in my employ several years ago at the Wyandanch Hotel. Your husband, Michael, came to the hotel asking for you. He said, "I recently made the passage back to New York from the gold rush. The new tenants at my wife's old address in Sag Harbor said that she and her family were gone, probably to the gold rush." He also said, "I checked her other employer, the Nassau Hotel, in vain and did not know where else to look. My old whale mates went to the gold rush or are at sea, and I had no one else to ask." I must admit, I felt sorry for him.

Your husband said, "If I do not have any luck locating my wife, I will conclude my search in the next few days. The whaling bark, *Neva*, docked at the wharf, is in need of crew, and I will join." Soon after he left, one chambermaid spoke of receiving a letter from Ellen Heffernan, of whom we were all fond. By then, it was too late to tell Michael I might have a lead, as he had already sailed.

A few weeks later, I received a letter from your husband with the return address, Faial Azores Island. Inside the envelope was another letter addressed to you. Your husband asked me to forward it to you if I ever found your whereabouts. I obtained your address from Ellen's friend. I am sorry if this is bad news for you, dear. I felt it my duty to pass the letter along.

Sincerely,
Mrs. Young

Letter from Catherine

155 Hudson Street
New York City
December 9, 1856

Dear Jane,

I am struggling to follow your advice despite a recent shock. Michael came back to your area looking for me. He knew better than to ask Tor, his avowed enemy, for my whereabouts. Why he did not think to look for you is a mystery. It is indeed ironic that the boys warned me that Michael would eventually return to the sea. They proved themselves right, while I was wrong. "You do not understand my husband," I insisted to them. Still deep inside, I recognized his restlessness back during his shipbuilding days for what it was: the sailor's itch.

I recall the gist of a yarn you once told me: "A seaman is a separate breed who hears a siren call the rest of us are deaf to. Their feet are leaden on dry land and need movement beneath them. It lulls them into comfort, like a mother rocking a baby in a cradle." Beneath my denial, I understood Michael would be helpless when the call captured him again. I was afraid to admit my fear that when my formidable rival, the sea, reasserted her hold, I would be left jilted. She herself had a rival in gold, even though the sea was the path to it.

When he sailed away this time from Greenport, I grasped the finality that I would never see Michael again in this life. There was nothing to base this belief on, but I knew it as well as my name. I remain unsurprised that he fulfilled my brothers' prophecy. Despite that, I still feel terrible guilt that he crossed the entire country to find me. It must have been awful for him. However, I did not ask him to do so, especially after staying away for so long.

I have a different life now, and I cannot return to being the Irish lass he remembered. For quite a while, I felt something died in me when I lost the baby, and I was alone. Upon much reflection, I realize something was born in me at the same time. Listening to myself has become a habit that I cannot cease. At first, it was a distant memory from the Irish Society School when my mind was so strong.

With practice my ability has returned, and I do not want to give it up. I also never wish to see the look on Michael's face when he learns of our loss. In return, I would not wish him to see mine when he finds no forgiveness. Finally, I have a confession to make. I have a letter from him in my possession that came by way of my old employer at the Wyandanch Hotel. I have locked it away in my hope chest, unread, where it will remain so. Of this, I am not proud, Jane.

Your friend,
Catherine

Letter from Jane

Division Street
Sag Harbor, New York
January 5, 1857

Dear Catherine,

With this news, you are like a hurt deer. Yet, like the animal, you will recover if the wound is not too deep. As you are on your feet, moving, your distress is being walked away. Even more, you are finding your true nature as you travel on your path. Keep walking on it. I am doing the same, and it works for me.

The letter under lock and key may be out of sight, but it will never be out of mind. Yet, to know it is there is different from knowing its contents. Only you can unravel that web between fact, hope, fear, and dread. There is no clock and you will act in your own time. When that time has come, however long it takes, you will know. Try to be at peace with it until then.

I have bought two more books for my collection: *The Scarlet Letter* and *Uncle Tom's Cabin*. Old Mr. Mulford is too sick to stay in his house, so he may move in with his youngest daughter. What that means for me, I cannot say. We are both trying to find our way ahead and with guidance, we will.

Your friend,
Jane

SUSAN MCGUIRK

Letter from Frank

Rose Farm
Hayground
Bridgehampton, New York
January 16, 1857

Dear Cath,

It must have been grim to learn that Michael returned to Sag Harbor looking for you. With the village hollowed out after the gold rush and the decline of the whale fishery, of course, he found no one he used to know. Even if he had come to Bridgehampton, I doubt he would have heard about me toiling on this godforsaken farm out in the backwoods. That he came out this way shows a devotion to you on Michael's part.

I also heard about him joining the crew of the *Bark Neva*, so now I know Michael went back on his vow to reject the sea. That I predicted as much does not make me feel justified, only sad. There are no winners in this story. It has been a long time, and as your brother, I can say this. I have seen you be mean sometimes, but I have never known you to be vindictive. Even though Saint Colmcille's Bell of Vengeance was entrusted to our family to keep and watch over, it does not mean we subscribe to its warring origins.

Colmcille was a displaced scholar, expelled from Ireland to the island of Iona, just as you are a displaced scholar in New York. He presided over the monks of his order in the monastery, copying civilization's most precious texts in Greek, Latin, and Hebrew. Consider our family's esteemed patron, Cath, and how he and his monks used writing to save culture, as you must use writing to save your soul. Now is the time to vanquish your vendetta and finally reply to Michael.

Yours forever,
Frank

Letter from Susie, in Gaelic

Tomasina Farm
Scuttle Hole Road

Bridgehampton, New York
May 15, 1857

Dear Cath,
    I am sorry to say that I have become a holder of a book, *The Pathfinder*. There is a letter inside addressed to you from Hawaii. It came by way of a voyage on the *Bark Byron*. My brother Charles sailed on it with his crewmate, Joe Josey. The vessel had a gam in Hawaii with the *Bark Neva* that Michael served on. I have not read the letter, but I was told Joe wrote it about Michael. The letter is still in the book, but I can no longer keep it for you.
    My cousin Betsey Fee is now married to Joe Josey. He is older than she, but Betsey can use his calming ways with her wild ideas. She is like her mother, Aunt Bridget, who thought she could tell the cotton factory how to spin. I wish I could help, but I cannot get in the middle of a family fuss. I will leave *The Pathfinder* with Frank for you. It may be a sign that this book and letter have traveled across many seas and hands. Perhaps now is the time to think about Michael more mercifully, Cath.

Your oldest friend,
Susie

You shall no longer take things second or third hand, nor look
through the eyes of the dead, nor feed on the spectres in books,
You shall not look through my eyes either, nor take things from me,
You shall listen to all sides and filter them from yourself.

"Song of Myself," 2
Leaves of Grass
Walt Whitman

Chapter Six

1857–1860

Letter from Catherine

155 Hudson Street
New York City
December 12, 1857

Dear Frank,

    When Mr. Bechet ushered me into his drawing room one afternoon, I thought it was to finally promote me to the role of governess. Instead, he announced that the family would return to Paris next spring. My life instantly turned topsy-turvy. His words about a Panic were a jumble in my ears. There was insufficient gold or silver to back up the money in circulation. A shipwreck and telegraph were involved. I could not discern his reasoning, just that he meant this part of my life was over.

    I thought about my darling Delphina, now ten years old, and how we would never see each other again. My present state of equilibrium and peace has been long sought and cherished. After contributing so much to this family, it was shattering to be left at their doorstep. Teaching the children has meant everything to me. Despair enveloped me as my knees slowly weakened. I clung to the wing chair next to me to keep from fainting.

    The bells clanging brightly from Saint John's Chapel entered my addled head. It startled me enough to remind me they meant something. It was the words from your last letter, ringing along with the chimes in my ear. They brought back Da's voice: "We are the Keepers of the Bell of Saint Colmcille. In times of trial, remember the Duty and Honor of the Bell."

The prolonged tolling continued, along with the recollection of our patron's command. My back slowly stiffened, and I was upright once more on my shaking legs. I would have to begin again. I must summon a new quest out of the ruins of this position or relinquish my dream forever. The bells continued to peal loudly. They ring for us all, Frank.

Yours forever,
Cath

Letter from Delphina Bechet

155 Hudson Street
New York City
March 21, 1858

Dear Madame,

Knowing I will lose you soon, these last months have been the worst of my life. I am so grateful that you have been my true and only teacher. You are my best friend, and I cannot live without you, dearest Madame.

I am begging my parents to send me to boarding school in the United States instead of France. I cannot bear to have an ocean between us. If only you could come to Paris with me. I do not want to live without you, Madame.

Your own,
Delphina

Letter from Catherine

155 Hudson Street
New York City
May 11, 1858

Dear Patrick,

Once again, I turn to you when I have a problem. A better friend would write inquiring about the health of your family without the excuse of asking for help. By now, you are used to my ways and, improbably, always overlook the drama, and for that, I thank you. This letter is no exception. I have lost my position, as my employers are leaving the country. I must start again and am looking to you, as always, for advice.

I am loath to admit that I am truly at my wits' end this time. I believed the Bechets would help me secure another position. They have yet to make any provisions for me, as they are caught up in their preparations to move to Paris. While I can still reside in their home for the time being, I am floundering, searching for employment. Positions are few during this time of financial hardship.

With a heavy heart and after much reflection, I have decided to book a passage home to Ireland. I will stay with my uncle and probably teach at his school. Going there is preferable to returning to my family in Long Island as the burdensome spinster sister.

I am trying not to feel bitter and to stop blaming myself. The time has passed for me to regret my decisions. Being alone is my doing, and I must admit defeat with good grace. No longer can I drag Michael's sister Ellen behind me like a ball and chain. I do not have the strength, even if my promise to Michael remains unfulfilled. I will be fortunate just to save myself. You are among the wisest people I know, and any counsel from you will help. I do hope Mickey, Julia, and you are well.

Your penfriend,
Catherine

SUSAN MCGUIRK

Letter from Patrick

129 Cedar Street
New York City
June 17, 1858

Dear Catherine,

Please do nothing you will regret. I do have an idea for you, but there is something I must tell you first. We lost little Mickey to scarlet fever. How God could take our innocent little boy is beyond my human reckoning. I, too, caught the fever but have recovered.

Unfortunately, because of the damage to my heart, I can no longer travel or even labor at an office. We are relegated to living off my savings, which, thankfully, may be enough. Our family has moved from the suite on Water Street to a boarding house on Cedar Street. Julia has no complaint about our reduction in circumstances and compared to our grief, it means little to me either. We just try to journey from one day to the next.

I have not forgotten my offer of assistance. I met a family in our new building who recently moved their fur trading business from Canada to New York. They are an extended family with five young cousins, headed by Joseph Bose and his widowed sister. They require a governess to teach the children. The family are Metis people, meaning half French and half Algonquin, who speak a dialect called Michif. They require a French speaker to be understood. It took me aback when they mentioned the requirement, as if the position had your name on it.

Even though our children are lost to us, Catherine, maybe, in turn, these children have found you. If you decide to pursue the position, write to Mr. Bose at the above address. As your wise friend Walt Whitman said so long ago, "Live in Manhattan. You belong there."

Your penfriend,
Patrick

Letter from Joseph Bose, in French

129 Cedar Street
New York City
October 26, 1858

Dear Mrs. Heffernan,

I am responding to you to introduce myself and help you understand our reasons for coming to New York. The fur trade has declined in New France since the Panic of 1857. A series of restrictive laws were passed that ordered us to deny that we are native people. We could only speak English or French, never our dialect, Michif. They vowed in writing to take away our culture and traditions.

We are proud Métis, and our fur business has survived for a hundred years despite the vagaries of the trade. New York has become our home, and we will rebuild our trading business as before. Is there a Mr. Heffernan? I speak for our whole family when I ask for your help and guidance. Please accept the position of our children's governess.

Respectfully yours,
Joseph Bose

Letter from Catherine, in French

155 Hudson Street
New York City
November 4, 1858

Dear Mr. Bose,

With utmost gratitude, I accept your offer of employment as a governess to the children in your family. I am honored and pleased to teach them French literature, English language and literature, history, geography, mathematics, and science.

Thank you for this opportunity, and I promise to perform my duties to the best of my ability. Thank you again, and I will not disappoint you. In answer to your question, there is no Mr. Heffernan. My husband left for the gold rush in 1848 and did not return.

Yours truly,
Catherine M. Heffernan

Letter from Ellen, in Gaelic

155 Hudson Street
New York City
November 29, 1858

Dear Cath,

I will be lost without you. We were together so long that I forgot what life was like without you by my side. My brother left me in your hands, but you were always kind. You treated me like a real sister, something neither of us had, and I hope I was one to you. How proud I was that you were the matron of honor at my marriage to James Burke. You were my only kin there.

Thank goodness the Burke brothers lived in your new building, and you introduced me to them. I might have remained a spinster forever. To the other chambermaids, I said, "The trick to finding a husband is a sister moving to a boarding house where three Irish brothers live."

I am nervous about moving to Pennsylvania to live with his parents, but James says the countryside is lovely there. Good luck in your new position as a governess with the Bose family. I am so happy for you that your dream finally came true. You will be the mistress of your very own little school. Congratulations, Cath. Also, have no fear. The secret of your whereabouts will remain safe with me. Even if I wished to, I do not know where my brother is to tell him.

Your almost sister,
Ellen

Letter from Catherine, in Gaelic

129 Cedar Street
New York City
December 4, 1858

Dear Ellen,

Thank you for your sweet letter. I send my best wishes to you and James for a long and happy life together. I am so pleased that you have found your beloved. You never stopped believing you would be lucky in love and your wish is fulfilled. I am sure the Burke family will accept you with open arms, and you will love country life.

Before we part for good, I hope you believe I do not hate Michael. I might have resented him for a while, but not now. It makes me feel old and tired to think of how much time has passed. Our romance was so sweet and fleeting, as though it happened to other people long ago. I can no longer summon Michael's face or voice clearly in my memory.

I remember the joy of young love and feel grateful I had that opportunity, however momentary. It was not my destiny to have a happy home and be cared for by a loving husband. Your destiny is to be cherished by James, and you so deserve it. As someone who always thinks of others, you will have a turn to be treasured by your new family.

I am sorry that I was selfish and wanted my way. I was callous to you, and I hope you can forgive me. Being a mother was a calling I missed, but I hope you will be blessed as one, Ellen.

Your almost sister,
Cath

Letter from Patrick, under the door

129 Cedar Street
New York City
December 11, 1858

Dear Catherine,

Congratulations on the position with the Bose family. I know what becoming a governess means to you, almost better than anyone. After all, you were only eighteen when you confided your ambition to me. Even though you are now thirty-four years old, I consider your accomplishment of this aspiration admirable and timely. You spent many years teaching and developing your skills, and this is the culmination. How fitting it is for you, with a resonance that seems justified and satisfying.

I welcome you to the building and look forward to finally enjoying a friendship sans paper. We missed each other in person for too long. You may ask yourself, "Why is Patrick still writing to me now that we are neighbors?" There is one caveat to continuing our friendship face-to-face, and her name is Julia. I am afraid that she is rather jealous of you. She knows nothing of our penfriendship but senses we are more than passing acquaintances.

I told her, "Catherine is an old family friend, and I knew her brothers." The statement is mostly valid, but it will not take much to raise her suspicions. Perhaps we can limit our meetings to exchanges on the staircase, where we "happen" to encounter each other. You also still have the option of leaving a letter for me in the hallway box. I apologize in advance for this unforeseen wrinkle in our planned reunion. I am making strides in my health with my physical heart, but my aching emotional heart only manages small steps. Seeing you will help.

Your penfriend,
Patrick

~

Letter from Catherine, left in the hallway box

129 Cedar Street
New York City
December 18, 1858

Dear Patrick,

I understand Julia's hesitation and respect the boundaries of polite society. Unrelated men and women do not address one another at length. I will adhere to propriety and never put you in a difficult position. As your wife, Julia has every right to expect nothing less, and I will not disappoint either of you.

I hoped, perhaps naively, that your wife and I could become friendly acquaintances at least. Now I see how unlikely that prospect is. I will politely keep my distance and only respond beyond a cordial greeting when I am spoken to. Any woman fortunate enough to marry you would feel the same. If I were in Julia's place, the situation would not be comfortable to me either.

Trust me, Patrick, you will never know how much a wave, a glance, or a short greeting will mean to me. It is more than enough and much more than we have ever had. I will treasure every meeting between us, however transitory. After so long on paper, thank you for allowing me into your life in the flesh.

Your penfriend,
Catherine

Letter from Catherine

129 Cedar Street
New York City
December 30, 1858

Dear Tor,

Please allow me to explain what fine people the Bose family are. They are descendants of distinguished French settlers who came to the New World in the 1600s. When these men came from France, they married Algonquin women. Their descendants became known as the Métis, meaning mixed people. The family is employed in the fur trade, has a good livelihood, and can pay decent wages. I have been furnished with a perfectly adequate room.

They are a family of respectable parents who are devoted to their children. Their religion is the same as ours, and they were also treated horribly by the English. I am finally a governess and using my French once again for my profession. I have worked for this and deserve it.

Your loving sister,
Cath

SUSAN MCGUIRK

Letter from Tor

Tomasina Farm
Scuttle Hole Road
Bridgehampton, New York
January 31, 1859

Dear Cath,

    I hate always being in the position of admonishing you. However, as the man of the family in this country, I am responsible for your well-being. Mam and Da would expect nothing less. That is why I must question your residence with this family.

    I understand you have always wanted to be an actual governess. You have had a long and pleasant association as a private teacher, which should be enough. To start all over again with new people when you should be with your family is wrong. Your nieces and nephews could benefit from your teaching prowess, and I would be happy to pay. There is a place divinely ordained for women to live among family. My responsibility is to protect you. Please do not condemn me for doing just that.

    I ask you to cease this arrangement and return to your family on the farm. The truth is harsh and challenging, but for the best, dear sister. You live with strangers whose true natures have yet to be revealed. As Michael has fulfilled your brothers' prediction and must be considered permanently absent, we are the only family you have now. Please accept your fate and understand there is nothing wrong with coming home to your folk. When we next write to each other, I hope for better news on our impending reconciliation.

Your brother,
Tor

Letter from Johnny

Woodruff Farm
Hayground
Bridgehampton, New York
February 17, 1859

Dear Cath,

By now, I am sure you have turned a deaf ear to Tor's ranting. You know he means well. The three of you left Ireland when you could, just as I did. He still feels guilty for leaving me behind, as if there was a choice. Your separation in New York reminds him of that guilt, that is all. He is doing his best for all of us.

My refuge when I am at liberty from laboring on this farm is in their kitchen, at the corner of Scuttle Hole Road and Brick Kiln Road in Bridgehampton. Tor's farm is up to thirteen acres, with several more in grazing land, and is flourishing. He asked me, "Please help me bring these crops to market next week: ten bushels of potatoes, eighteen bushels of buckwheat, thirty-five bushels of oats, five pounds of butter, and twenty dozen eggs." I felt proud to help him and appreciate all the assistance he has given. Tor helps not only me but also all the new Irish people who regularly come to the area. Someday, I would like people to look up to me with the same respect our oldest brother commands.

My new farmhand position does not pay much, but I save every spare penny to buy a farm someday. Luckily, our big brother feeds me when my wages dwindle from saving so much. You are doing what is right for you, Cath, and no one can say otherwise. Congratulations on fulfilling your lifelong dream of becoming a governess. I am very proud of you, dear sister.

Your younger brother,
Johnny

SUSAN MCGUIRK

Letter from Francis

Tomasina Farm
Scuttle Hole Road
Bridgehampton, New York
March 18, 1859

Dear Aunt Cath,

    I do not blame you for staying in New York. Now that I am big, thirteen years old, I understand things, maybe more than my pa does. Like my uncle Charles Fee, I want to have a different life. He was a seaman in a family of farmers who loved adventure and travel. Those are things I want to do.

    When I am older, I will visit you in New York City. I will show you my drawings if Pa has not thrown them away. He disapproves of boys who draw pictures. Next year, I will begin my apprenticeship as a blacksmith. I have my ideas about smithing, but I will wait until I have learned the trade to test them. My farm chores call, as I am already in trouble for the tasks I failed to finish. I miss you, Auntie, and I hope you will return to see us.

Your favorite nephew,
Francis

Letter from Catherine

129 Cedar Street
New York City
June 25, 1859

Dear Frank,

    Living on a farm, away from your family, is a difficult adjustment. I, too, am adapting, but this may finally be the chance I have waited for. My new neighborhood is not the sanctuary that the Saint John's Park area was. The intersection of Cedar and Williams Streets is a drastic reversal from the glamour and luxury of my previous address. However, we are still many blocks from the notorious neighborhood you remember, the Five Points, and no gangs are active in the area. The building's exterior and interior are unadorned and a bit run-down. At least, we are only five blocks from the New York Commons, an enormous park for the children to play in.

My room is no smaller than the one at the Bechet house, but a bit spartan and not as warm. At least I am comfortable enough, and I have my privacy. I only confide this to you, Frank, but the family's ability to pay me is scarcely more than Ellen's last salary. However, their abiding belief in education helps mitigate that drawback. They want their children to learn, improve, and make a place for themselves in this new world, as do I.

Here, I am treated with a respect I never quite felt with the Bechet family. I have reached a higher station as a governess, but that is not all. It is my responsibility to choose the children's lesson plans and fashion their education as I see fit. I am using my talents in the service of my chosen profession. It may be the best feeling I have ever had in my life. Love to you, Isabella, and Mamie.

Yours forever,
Cath

Letter from Frank

Rose Farm
Hayground
Bridgehampton, New York
July 20, 1859

Dear Cath,

Tor is not your master, and you do not have to listen to him. He lives a sheltered life as a farmer and lacks familiarity with the varied folks we know. He regularly visits Sag Harbor to sell his crops, but besides his family, Tor mostly talks to horses, cows, and chickens. That is why I dislike living on this farm. Give me fellowship and a stroll to the tavern for a pint of ale in good company any day.

I am unfamiliar with the Métis from Canada, but they sound like fine folk. Maybe you can send me one of those fur hats they sell for the cold winter. I could use some extra warmth while tilling and hoeing in the bitter winds.

Isabella will still not leave the almshouse. She continues to slip further away from us, and we can do nothing to halt her retreat. I truly dread the day Mamie and I visit Isabella when she does not recognize us. I fear it will not be long. Be well in your latest new life, Cath, my girl. You set your mind to this purpose long ago, and through persistence and determination, you fulfilled it. Well done, Madam Governess!

Yours forever,
Frank

Letter from Susie, in Gaelic

Tomasina Farm
Scuttle Hole Road
Bridgehampton, New York
August 4, 1859

Dear Cath,

Congratulations on your new position. I always knew your dream of being a governess would come true. Now that baby Lillie has arrived, I am with child again. I am not sure whether to laugh or cry. I thought my time was over, as I am getting on in years. Tor is happy with the news and says it is a blessing. This had better be the last one, or I may drown in blessings. At least the older children help me, especially Minnie. When Francis does not have his head in a cloud, he can be helpful and good company for me. He told me the other day, "Mother, someday I will be a famous artist of iron."

I told him, "There is no such trade."

"There soon will be," he said.

Tor and Francis are often arguing, but he makes me laugh with his strange ideas.

Sometimes I pretend to myself that I get on a train to visit you in New York. We link arms and wander through the park, enjoying the fine weather and catching up on our gossip. We have on our stylish day dresses, not fancy but spun of fine wool, not thin cotton. Our bonnets have ribbons and bows, while our gloves are made of lace. As we stroll, we smile at all the nursemaids trying to gather the children running about.

Maybe pretending is my grown-up version of the two of us blowing down the hill together in Mullinclavin. It helps me with all the whining, squabbling, colic, and such. I need a daily dose of make-believe to get through the day. Even though I am not going anywhere, the idea of running off, like down a hill, helps. Writing to you helps as well.

Your oldest friend,
Susie

Letter from Delphina, in French

Paris
Île de France, France
August 5, 1859

Dear Madame,
   Now my secret is revealed. I can hardly recall my English, and no one here speaks it with me. My parents behave as though we never lived in America. The girls at school are unkind to me and say I have a terrible accent and read too many books. Mama says they are jealous of me, but I think they dislike me because I lived in New York.
   I still miss it, but most of all, I miss you. It is not the same without you. I stopped singing and dancing, and they say I am shy. The sun does not shine without my Madame. It frightens me that the sound of your voice and your sweet smile are becoming distant in my memory. When I grow up, I will come and live with you again. How can I wait so long when I cannot stop missing you?

Your,
Delphina

SUSAN MCGUIRK

Letter from Catherine, in Gaelic

129 Cedar Street
New York City
August 27, 1859

Dear Susie,

    I am sending you strength and endurance in your impending role as the mother of six children. You are indeed blessed. Your shining attitude and sense of amusement will win the day. You will turn the chores into a game the children will compete to help with. In addition, Francis and Minnie will be old enough to step up and be the help you need.
    I reside in a boarding house on Cedar Street, where my employers rent a floor of rooms. There are whalemen and mariners here and a plumber, baker, shoemaker, and tailor, several of whom are Irish. However, just before moving here, a notorious and murderous pirate, Albert Hicks, lived in the building, though he was already in prison when I arrived. The news of his crimes had been in the newspapers for weeks. I would have lost my nerve to go forward if he had not gone. One resident of the building is a gentleman I met aboard the *Queen Victoria* on our passage seventeen years ago. What a pleasant coincidence, I must say.
    The extended family I am employed by has five cousins to teach. We have a classroom set up among the rooms they let, which makes me feel like a professional schoolmistress. I was nervous about understanding my charges' dialect at first. We soon conversed freely since Michif is a version of their French ancestors' language. I especially enjoy having the long-denied opportunity to teach arithmetic and science to the children, particularly the girls.
    That I am still struggling in this unfamiliar situation makes me impatient with myself. Maybe I miss Delphina, and Ellen, more than I admit. This neighborhood is gritty and grimy and frightens me occasionally, like when a vagrant followed the children and me. He shouted, "Savages" at them and "Biddy" at me, which was very disturbing.
    At least I can withdraw from the tumult beyond the windows of my small classroom. Outside, in the streets of New York, prejudice against me, my charges, and my employers is ever present. Within our four walls, we are free to learn, think, and study. It erases the raucous, sometimes hostile clamor that is life on the streets of this neighborhood.

Being free to teach the children as I see fit is indeed a rare and joyful treasure for which I am very grateful.

Your oldest friend,
Cath

Letter from Catherine, in French

129 Cedar Street
New York City
September 29, 1859

Dear Delphina,

Never fear, my dear. I am happy to respond to you in any language. I am glad you are still reading, but I am sorry that the girls can be unpleasant. When I was your age, the girls were not nice to me either. I was separate from the other students as one of the only Catholics at my school, and I still remember how it felt. They may ridicule you for being different, but you should be proud of who you are. You can tell them, "I consider myself lucky that I am a world traveler, and I wish you the same opportunity."

Adversity, as painful as it can be, is also a time of discovery. If you can be patient and believe that things will get better, they usually do. Even when patience is not enough, hardship gives us choices. We can try fighting back. Avoiding the situation is another common approach. Rising above unacceptable behavior by simply not engaging may be the best choice.

The point is to keep trying. If we can move forward, we have already won. Defeat stands still while success stays in motion. Please do not give up, my darling.

I would love to live with you anywhere, anytime. Perhaps we will someday, but until then, I will miss you each day.

Your loving,
Madame

SUSAN MCGUIRK

Letter from Patrick, left under the door

129 Cedar Street
New York City
September 9, 1861

Dear Catherine,

By now, you will have heard that I volunteered for the War of the Rebellion. I am sorry that I left without saying goodbye. I knew if anyone could stop me, it would be you. Your opinion has always been high in my esteem. Before the volunteer process becomes more entrenched, I acted with haste to avoid a more thorough medical examination.

I am not sure how to justify my decision to serve. The only way I can make you understand is for you to consider it my last stand. I did it for my boys, even though my little lost Mickey will never know. When baby Jay grows up, he will know his father served his adopted home, where we are free from the oppression that we both endured.

Becoming a citizen was one of my proudest moments, and my son will serve as a native-born American someday. Volunteering is something I believe I am summoned for, despite the condition of my heart. Please try to understand, Catherine. It would mean a lot to me.

Your penfriend,
Patrick

Letter from Catherine, left in the hallway box

129 Cedar Street
New York City
September 27, 1861

Dear Patrick,

I will swallow my objections and support your decision to serve in the War of the Rebellion. However, I may never be at peace with it. Instead, I will try to aid Julia with little Jay, even if I risk being rebuffed. I will also pray for your health and safe return.

Good luck with the rest of your training, and please do not push yourself. While you have shown improvement in your stamina, promise me you will ask for accommodations from your commanding officers. Look for me waving my handkerchief when your regiment parades to the wharf. I will be the woman standing alone, full of pride and hope.

Your penfriend,
Catherine

Letter from Patrick

65th Regiment, Company C
Malvern Hill, Virginia
July 9, 1862

Dear Catherine,

I look forward to coming home, although I know you are still not satisfied with my explanations for volunteering. You tried to understand, which meant so much to me. In my condition, my participation in the war would always be short-lived.

I am crestfallen but not surprised that my superiors are sending me home after a few months. I am also relieved, as I have struggled to keep up. My official discharge record will be for "disability" after our latest battle in Malvern Hill, Virginia. Being discharged is no shame, but it is not how anyone wants to depart. Still, I am grateful that I could serve and will be a proud war veteran.

Your penfriend,
Patrick

SUSAN MCGUIRK

Letter from Catherine

129 Cedar Street
New York City
September 12, 1862

Dear Patrick,

    I am so thankful that you are being mustered out of the army. This has been a long few months worrying about your health and well-being. I still cannot imagine how you were accepted with your damaged heart. So many are shirking the army's call. You stepped forward at the very outset at greater risk to yourself than almost anyone. It will be a pleasure to see you back in the building.

    I must admit that Julia has seemed deeply worried. Not that she would share her concerns with me, as she continues to keep her distance. Yet I have seen her pained expression, and the lines on her face begin to set. Thank goodness for little Jay, who lifts her spirits. Hurry home, dear friend.

Your penfriend,
Catherine

The smallest sprout shows there is really no death,
And if ever there was it led forward life, and does not wait at the end to arrest it,
And ceas'd the moment life appear'd.
All goes onward and outward, nothing collapses,
And to die is different from what any one supposed, and luckier.

"Song of Myself," 6
Leaves of Grass
Walt Whitman

Chapter Seven

1861–1866

Letter from Frank

Rose Farm
Hayground
Bridgehampton, New York
November 16, 1862

Dear Cath,

The army has finally come to recruit in Bridgehampton. I volunteered for the War of the Rebellion from the North District, so this is soon to be a farewell. Johnny joined me, but was chagrined when they sent him home for being underweight. It was only a few pounds, but he was distraught and blamed it on the famine. I will sorely miss having him by my side.

What an honor to be among Duryea's Zouaves. Colonel Abram Duryea of the 7th New York State Militia founded the regiment, named after a famous French version. They select educated, tall, and strong men. Some lads have already served in European armies, while others are college men, lawyers, and businessmen. I am proud to be in the army's finest regiment and ready to defeat the Confederates.

We are sailing to Louisiana, the home of New Orleans. I may get a fine French meal there, *n'est-ce pas, ma cherie?* Please do not fret over me, sister dear. Of course, I considered my girls before volunteering for the war, and I am going for them. I can make more money in this godforsaken army than I can as a lowly farmhand. This is a better way to provide for my family, as I was never much of a farmer.

I hope you do not mind that I brought your copy of Herman Melville's *Typee* to read aboard the ship. Who better to read than your old friend on a sea voyage? It was in a box of old books with your name on it. My parting wish is that you write back to your poor husband. I would love to think of you finally being at peace with the situation. As I always say to you, "When I hear you laugh, the angels sigh." No matter what happens, I will miss you.

Yours forever,
Frank

Letter from Mamie

Hayground
Corwith Farm
Bridgehampton, New York
November 20, 1862

Dear Aunt Cath,

I know you are going to the wharf to see Pa's ship off. I wish to tell him something I did not get a chance to say before he left. I am fourteen years old now, and just as boys say they are the man of the family, well, I am the woman of my family now. Tell Pa I will find a way to care for Ma, and he needn't worry. I am old enough to find a trade and do chores at the farm beside Uncle Johnny. I hope Pa will not be gone long. I do not know much about wars, but I wish he were not going. One of these days I hope to visit you in the city. I have always wanted to go there.

Your niece,
Mamie

Letter from Tor

Tomasina Farm
Scuttle Hole Road
Bridgehampton, New York
December 2, 1862

Dear Cath,

Isabella died on December 1. We feared the worst, but she was so frail that no one could be sure what happened. The life in her seemed to seep out when she heard Frank left. It took only two weeks from his sailing to Louisiana for us to lose her. Regardless of whether her death was intentional, from sickness, or caused by a broken heart, she has already been buried. Isabella left a note with the words, "I must see Angelina. She misses me." No one understands what it means.

With Frank at sea, it may be months before he learns the truth. We are making plans for Mamie to become our ward. Frank thought he was solving his problems by volunteering, but he was really fleeing from them.

Your loving brother,
Tor

Letter from Catherine

129 Cedar Street
New York City
December 10, 1863

Dear Mamie,

I send you my deepest condolences for your beloved mother's parting. The present appears bleak, but I promise you will survive this loss. I was there when you were born, and your mama loved you so much. She was too beautiful, sensitive, and sweet for this harsh world. I would ascribe those attributes to you, dear Mamie, but you are also plucky, energetic, and brave, like your pa. Those traits will enable you to find your way through life, no matter how difficult.

You are stronger than your lovely ma and will not succumb to her fate. With your pa gone to the war, you will be fine with your uncles and cousins and will never be alone with your family around you. When Pa comes home, the two of you will live happily together once more. I gave him your message at the wharf before he sailed to Louisiana. He was thinking of you as the ship pulled away from the pier. I will pray for your strength to face this sad time and go forward.

Your loving aunt,
Cath

Letter from Catherine

129 Cedar Street
New York City
March 15, 1863

Dear Jane,

With so many young men leaving for the war, it feels like the gold rush again. By now, you have heard about your neighbor's volunteering. Frank looked impressively handsome in his Zouave uniform in the daguerreotype he sent me. I am proud that he will serve his adopted country. Still, I cannot shake a sense of dread about the whole business.

I wonder whether Michael, someplace in the world, is also being drawn into this war. Like other women, I volunteer to roll bandages for the troops on the battlefield. I need a task that makes me feel less helpless. The entire country is slowly being consumed by death and destruction. Stay strong, dear friend.

Your friend,
Catherine

Letter from Catherine, left in the hallway box

129 Cedar Street
New York City
July 12, 1863

Dear Patrick,

I am sorry to burden you with this news by letter. I cannot bring myself to speak the words in one of our brief encounters. As you are a veteran and dear friend, my sentiments will fall on sympathetic ears. My brother Frank's regiment, the 165th Infantry, was sent to Louisiana aboard an army ship. Their first order of business was to protect the mouth of the Mississippi River at Port Hudson, Louisiana. A few days into the battle, on May 27, 1863, our Frank was killed in action. My well-being has been shattered.

Now there is no dear one with whom I can share our childhood jokes. There is no brother to tease me, to make me laugh and forget my troubles for a little while. We will never again discuss our favorite books or recite poetry to each other. This splendid young man with so much promise and a family to care for was taken. His essence of high spirits, robust handsomeness, and the gift of spreading joy will not walk this way again.

Your penfriend,
Catherine

Letter from Tor

Tomasina Farm
Scuttle Hole Road
Bridgehampton, New York
July 18, 1863

Dear Cath,

By now, you have learned that our Frank has died. I offer the Gaelic blessing as he ascends to the pantheon with our beloved mam and da and our forebears. If only we could drink from the Bell of Colmcille to mend our broken hearts.

I fear that Johnny's grief is driving his decisions. He married Eliza Brennan, a girl he only briefly knew, claiming they were meant for each other. Then he turned around and re-registered in the Army, this time successfully. It is distressing news after losing Frank.

May I beseech you again, dear Cath? Please come home to us in our sorrow and turmoil. Your family needs you now more than ever. Young Mamie, and especially our young Francis, long for your presence. We are all missing you.

Your loving brother,
Tor

Letter from Catherine

129 Cedar Street
New York City
August 14, 1863

Dear Tor,

Perhaps the worst part of losing Frank is that his remains will never be recovered. We will never put flowers on his grave or offer prayers over it. All that was left of him was lost in action on a battlefield in Louisiana. What a place to die for a boy from County Monaghan. Frank had no business going there, let alone dying there. My grief has made me question our very immigration.

We came so far to escape tyranny, only to see our brother die for a cause he only assumed as his own. Frank told me this at the wharf before he sailed to the war. "We came here to seek freedom, not to protect those who deny it." He fought and died for us and for all those yearning to be free. I know I must not deny him his honor as an American, but I never imagined the sacrifice it would require.

Thank you for your kind and generous offer to join you in sorrow. It would be comforting to share this burden, but my position requires my presence here. Yet I appreciate that you are continually pointing me home. As much as I have resisted, you continue to be my rock, especially now that Frank is gone. I never forget there is a proverbial bed of hay below the barn rafter to catch me that you provide. I apologize if I seem cavalier toward your inclusive and heartfelt gestures.

I remember when the three of us had to get up early to milk cows and feed horses when we were young. Frank would throw feed at us, and you boys would try to knock over each other's milking stools. We had so many games to lift us against the drudgery when circumstances should have dragged us down, mostly made up by our lilting jester, Frank.

There is one approach I will employ to assuage my grief. While you may not agree with it, Frank's parting wish for me was to write to Michael. While I still struggle to fulfill it, I have put my wedding ring back on in Frank's honor. Our brother saved my life back in Mullinclavin with your help. If only we could have saved him.

Your loving sister,
Cath

Letter from Catherine, left in the hallway box

129 Cedar Street
New York City
March 12, 1864

Dear Patrick,

I have no one else to tell this news to who would not insist I leave New York at once. Only you will understand a recent shared experience that has deeply shaken my sense of security. I was almost trampled and threatened bodily during the recent riot in response to the draft here. I still cannot believe the sight of a mob of Irishmen. They were protesting being drafted to the war, marauding their way through the city.

My nightmare began when I was walking home from an errand. People began running down the street before me, shouting, "They are coming! Run! Hurry!"

I turned around and only saw more people running toward me. Suddenly, there were so many people that I found myself in the middle of a crowd. It surrounded me, and I was moved along involuntarily. I began running as well. I had trouble keeping pace with the charging crowd and feared being trampled if I fell. Soon I was engulfed in a throng holding torches of fire, shouting, "You will never take me! My life is worth more than three hundred dollars!"

Policemen appeared, trying to seize the surrounding men. They beat them with their truncheons, and one rioter grasped my waist.

I shouted, "Turn me loose!"

He replied, "Shut up!" and then called me an expletive I cannot repeat.

I gathered myself up and stared the man in the eye. "I am grieving for my war hero brother, and I will continue home with no further intervention!"

The ruffian looked startled and released me. I ran to Cedar Street as fast as possible and never looked back.

Your family's safety concerned me, but we were too frightened to emerge from our rooms until the next day. I looked for you in the hall, but it was empty. When we ventured outside, it seemed our neighborhood escaped the worst. The newspapers said the mob murdered over a hundred Black citizens and burned many buildings. President Lincoln pulled troops from the war into Manhattan to restore order. You and my brothers freely volunteered. The three of you could not differ more from your fellow Irishmen tearing apart our city.

You served at great personal sacrifice to your health, Patrick. My brother gave his life fighting for the country you both love. Some believe recent immigrants should not be drafted into the war when the native-born can pay to escape their duty. However, murdering innocent civilians is despicable. They seem like no countrymen of ours.

Your penfriend,
Catherine

Letter from Patrick left under the door

129 Cedar Street
New York City
March 14, 1864

Dear Catherine,

The riot was indeed a shock. I, too, could not believe our countrymen could behave this way. As I had not been feeling well, I missed all the excitement, although I could hear it in the distance. I am grateful that you are safe. I also hope you continue to recover from the loss of your dear brother.

While spending some time under the weather, I have been contemplating my life. It has been quite a journey so far, with many peaks and valleys. I had the unlikely opportunity to become a wealthy man. Without an income these past years, it is only a memory now. I never thought I would be a happily married family man, but that gift was given to me.

We remained compatriots through many upheavals. What a joy it has been to see you achieve your professional goals, Catherine. We have both accomplished more than we thought we would. That you are the mistress of your own small school and setting the lessons is truly admirable. When a young teenage girl shyly admitted that someday she wanted to be a governess, I believed in your chances. When Catherine says she will do something, it comes to pass.

Watching you struggle with your ambitions and setbacks over the years has not always been easy. There were many times when I yearned to ease your burden. It felt like my hands were tied with frustration. Still, you persevered and forged your way through your travails. For a long time, I did not understand that you were compelled to find your own path through the wilderness. Now I do. I had the same need, and I think you understood mine better.

Now we are older but not finished with our lives. I am sure fresh adventures await us as we embark on what is left of our futures. I have a front-row seat for the rest of your life.

Your penfriend,
Patrick

Letter from Jane

Eastville
Sag Harbor, New York
October 12, 1864

Dear Catherine,
It has been a while, but I offer my respects on the death of your dear brother. The whole Perdue family will miss him. Our nephew, George

Perdue, a whaleman, has registered for the United States Colored Troops. He says he must fight against slavery. I am so proud of him for that. The governor will not allow a regiment of the Colored Troops of America in New York. Some of our local men are enlisting in Connecticut. Our pastor at church, Rev. Thompson, has encouraged George to enlist there. Frederick Douglass, the Reverend's dear friend, has promised to speak to the regiment when they muster out.

I am sorry that your husband Michael has come from away like a jackal in the night. It stumps me that he would put a note in the newspaper looking for you. After so much time gone, it seemed your life with him was long over. You have a riddle with no simple answer. There could be something he wants from you, or maybe he wishes to make amends. Perhaps one or both of us will dream of it.

Mr. Mulford just passed away. We never became friends, but at the end of his life, we made peace. I am almost unwilling to admit it, but as he lay dying, I could see into his soul a bit. Maybe when he held my hand on his last day, he finally saw me as a person.

I now live with a whaleman and his wife, Charles and Mary Atkins. Charles is at sea, while Mary and I keep each other company and work at the church. I am happy to be among my people in this neighborhood of Eastville. No more must I parse every little step like I had to with Mr. Mulford. I am proud to say I have $350 in the Sag Harbor Savings Bank for my house to come. I continue to look for better-paying work, but times are hard with the whale fishery fading away. At least I can take in some washing, which helps.

Your friend,
Jane

༄

Letter from Catherine

129 Cedar Street
New York City
November 9, 1864

Dear Jane,

Thank you for your condolences. I sincerely hope you find the work you need now that your employment is gone. I am not especially proud to share this lesser concern with you, but that has never stopped me before. This is my question: "How would Jane react to Michael's query, looking for me after so long?" It would certainly not be with shaking hands and forgotten spectacles. Conjuring your presence helped me make a choice.

When I first sent you a copy of his advertisement in the Missing Friends notices, I reacted emotionally. However, upon reflection, I realize that no repercussions have occurred, and my life is not adversely affected. Therefore, I will pretend the advertisement never appeared unless events force me to reconsider.

I was content with my lot before I saw the newspaper. I will not allow it to disrupt me going forward. Here is what I am sure you will count as another of my Irish declarations: I banish Michael's words from my mind and will cease to consider them. I hope your book, china, and house funds can continue.

Your friend,
Catherine

*

Letter from Johnny

Briarpatch Farm
Brick Kiln Road
Bridgehampton, New York
November 29, 1864

Dear Cath,
It is a miracle that I have made it home. After surviving the Siege of Petersburg, I was so dulled that I stopped thinking and followed any order, no matter how horrible. My only solace was that Eliza was my wife, so I had someone to stay alive for. Without the dream of her, I would probably have given up. Marrying her before I left was the best decision I have ever made. About to be called up, I reflected upon how much of my time had been spent waiting, especially to cross the Atlantic Ocean. I did not want to spend another minute letting life pass by without seizing it. That is why I married and found a way to serve quickly.

I am relieved my service in the 57th Regiment, New York Infantry, is over. Thanks for your congratulations on the news of my impending fatherhood. That Frank is gone is still hard to accept. Each time I long for his advice, I grieve all over again. He and I planned to buy this farm to work together, but it was never to be. What good fortune that Eliza's dowry covered Frank's portion, so we could still make the purchase.

When I returned from the war, it fell upon me to pack up Frank's cabin at the Rose Farm. I found a box marked "Cath" with a few of your old books from the Division Street house. Sticking out of a copy of the book *The Pathfinder* was a letter addressed to you from Joe Josey. There is only one person the letter could be about. How unsettling that it appeared unbidden in Frank's possessions. Since I heard you put Michael's ring back on in Frank's honor, I will send you the book with the letter inside.

Your younger brother,
Johnny

Letter from Catherine

129 Cedar Street
New York City
January 3, 1865

Dear Johnny,

Please do not think ill of me. After so many years, I still suffer from paralysis over letters from Michael. Soon I will summon the courage to read this and the other letter I already possess. I will write to him but await the right frame of mind.

The previous letter from Michael, which he wrote from the Azores, is in my hope chest. Procrastination is my great failing, but I fully intend to read it. When you send it, I promise to read the letter in *The Pathfinder* as well.

Please try to understand my weakness and lack of resolve, Johnny. When Michael published his Missing Friends plea after so many years, it affected me much as Jane Perdue described: "Your husband has come from away like a jackal in the night." I am haunted and now hounded by Michael, and I simply want to be left alone in peace.

I have tried to force myself to behave more charitably toward him, but with few results. Now, you see the flawed woman I am, not the nurturing big sister you remember back in Ireland. That the paltry remains of Frank's worldly goods contained this message from the past is not lost on me. I will pay heed, I promise. I just need more time.

Your loving sister,
Cath

Letter from Susie, in Gaelic

Tomasina Farm
Scuttle Hole Road
Bridgehampton, New York
March 21, 1865

Dear Cath,

I still miss you often. Yet there is a little someone who eases my longing. Josephine is three years old and is the image of her Aunt Cath. She has your same golden-brown hair, bright blue eyes, and silly laugh. Everyone nicknamed her Jenny, but I still use her full name. It feels like I am back in Mullinclavin, playing with my wee best friend. Even her constant loud orders remind me of you. She is quickly becoming my other best friend, but please promise never to tell my other children.

Josephine and I play a game with our new litter of kids in the barn. It brings back the game we used to play with the lambs. Do you remember how we would take the smallest ones and hoist them on our shoulders? We would cuddle them in our arms like babies, and line them in a row to follow our footsteps through the grass. Our little feet were covered in mud and worse, which got us into trouble at home. Josephine and I even run down the sledding hill together, holding hands.

I still cannot believe I am the mother of so many children. Part of me feels like I am still growing up myself. I am afraid I am weak in correcting the children, and they know it. I must settle for being paid no heed, which is at least better than being laughed at. Fortunately, Tor's word is law, and the children obey when Pa speaks. Knowing the weight of my childbearing years has finally been lifted makes it easier to enjoy my last one.

Becoming a governess has lifted the weight you carried. You run a small school, which is rare for a woman. I do not know of another lady who is happily in charge while earning a salary.

I tell my girls about you so they will know women can do things besides motherhood. They can imitate you and get an education in something that only men know, like science. Maybe that long-ago row at the Women's Rights meeting was a bigger tug than you knew. Prepare to have the company of another woman in charge when young Josephine grows up.

Your oldest friend,
Susie

Letter from Ellen, in Gaelic

Indiana County
Blairsville, Pennsylvania
October 28, 1865

Dear Cath,

I miss you and hope you are well. It has been a while, but I have some news that may upset you. I recently found my brother by placing an advertisement in the Missing Friends notices. I have enclosed it for you below.

MISSING FRIENDS

OF MICHAEL, William and Eneas HEFFERNAN, natives of the parish of Cashel, county Tipperary, who lived in New York in the fall of 1848; when last heard from Eneas was in New York, and Michael and William in Weaversville,
Trinity county, California. Any information respecting them will be thankfully
Received by their sister, Mrs E Burke, Blairsville, Indiana county, Pennsylvania.

When Michael replied, he told me he had also placed an advertisement for you. He said you did not answer it. Maybe you do not wish to receive this news, but I am honor bound to tell you. This is what he wrote:

When I could not find Cathy year after year, I believed she must be dead. I started a new life and staked a claim on a homestead in Ohio. There, I married an older widow with three children whom I adopted. I became a citizen and served in the War.

I was wounded in an explosion on a battlefield and had a premonition that Cathy was still alive. That is why I placed the Missing Friends advertisement. I have a favor to ask. I entrust the enclosed letter I wrote to her from the Battle of Peachtree Creek in Atlanta to you. If my portent proves true and you cross paths with Cathy, would you give it to her?

Cath, I will send you Michael's letter only if you agree. He also fought in the Second Battle of Bull Run and Gettysburg. So many "missing friends" are just gone. Our brother William is one. He may be in California, on an island in the Pacific Ocean, or at the bottom of the sea. My brother Eneas took ill on the passage over and was soon dead.

I hope you are not reading this news alone. I am sending you love and strength.

Your almost sister,
Ellen

Letter from Catherine

129 Cedar Street
New York City
November 30, 1865

Dear Jane,

Once again, I turn to you. Ellen has informed me that Michael has a wife and family in Ohio. I have become numb upon hearing the news. I walk through the days in a trance, though I can perform my duties with outward calm. Inside, I am empty like I was in 1849 when my life took a tragic turn. I am afraid to feel anything. If I do, I might be at the bottom of another well, this time of regret and recrimination.

I dislike myself for resenting Michael, which is petty and beneath me. I wish I could quell these feelings. He did what anyone in his situation would do to continue pursuing a full life. If only this admission would make me more benevolent.

These waves continue to wash over me. Why does he bestow strangers with the loving family life he withheld from me? To make us both guilty of the crime of bigamy, even unintentionally, is the absolute nadir of our so-called marriage.

This floundering serves no purpose and will only hurt me and others, and I long for your presence. In Frank's memory, Michael's ring was returned to my finger. Now I imagine my foot stamping it into the wooden sidewalk. I will turn to teaching, my real savior, to be healed. Once again, I need to retreat into my lessons, books, and students to find a respite from the turmoil.

Your friend,
Catherine

Letter from Jane

Liberty Street
Eastville
Sag Harbor, New York
January 2, 1866

Dear Catherine,

You have suffered a nasty blow, Catherine. Please trust that your loss is not of a piece to Michael's gain. There can be two facts that do not meet. The river flows on a forked path, and neither branch will cross. You will soon accept this and heal as before, and it will not take long.

Time has been kind to me. Until recently, I was boarding with the pastor of the Saint David A.M.E. Zion Church and his wife while I continued my savings. When my Sag Harbor Savings Bank account reached five hundred dollars, I bought my house. It was hard to save so much, and I could not be prouder that I did it.

The small miracle is that the house is on Liberty Street. I know the spirits have blessed my home because the name of my street stands for all that my people and I have fought for. You should see it, Catherine. On a small lot sits a little wood-frame house with shingles and three bay windows. It has one story with a pitched roof. A front hall leads to four rooms—a parlor, a back room, a kitchen, and a bedroom. The rooms are mostly empty now, but someday, there will be furniture and shelves for my collections.

I receive rent from my new boarders, the Cuffee family. The money frees me to serve as a stewardess at Saint David, where I have always wanted to be a leader. Another promise I will make for my church is to put a fine headstone for Silas in the graveyard. Someday both our names will be carved on it.

The days when I left my letters to you in the shed are long gone. Now that there is little risk of them being seen by others, I can safely confess another reason that Saint David A.M.E. Zion Church means so much to me. It is a stop on what is called the Maritime Underground Railroad. Sag Harbor is a way station for runaway slaves stowed away on vessels from Southern ports. While they wait for the next voyage northward, the escaped slaves hide under a trapdoor in the church's pulpit. Everyone in our parish risks great danger and takes much pride in this worthy mission.

I had a dream about you last night. To remind you, the Algonquin people believe that a spiritual message is told and made whole in a dream. I dreamed a bird flew a long way to a new tree where another bird awaited. They began building a nest out of twigs, leaves, and straw.

I believe the bird was you, which means a journey to a new home, perhaps far away, may come soon. It may be a place you have never seen or visited, but you will make a home with someone you have been missing. I hope it means you will come back to Sag Harbor and live with me in my house. Please let your dreams speak more about this because it has left me now. Tell me what the spirits say to you.

Your friend,
Jane

SUSAN MCGUIRK

Letter from Catherine

129 Cedar Street
New York City
March 7, 1866

Dear Jane,

    I am elated that you have arrived at your life's goal of home ownership. How perfect that it is on Liberty Street. I can picture it from your description. A memory of me is on its way there, a copy of *Silas Marner* by George Eliot, for your bookshelf. The title is in honor of your dear late husband, and the surprise is that the author is a woman whose real name is Mary Ann Evans. The house may be empty now, but it will not be for long.

    It seems like a small miracle, yet your house was long planned and sacrificed for. It was far from inevitable, and only your unwavering belief and determination made it possible. Congratulations, my friend. Someday, I will visit your parlor. You will serve us tea on your lovely china, and we will browse your full bookshelf together.

    Your dream struck me as a bit unsettling. However, as nice a suggestion as it is, I do not foresee your new house as my destination. Trying to remember my dreams these last nights has been futile. If only your dream could stop me from grappling with the same old anger and resentments. I am trying to emulate your example and take your advice.

    For the first time, I am finally beginning to understand your teachings to me, Jane. You are so right. I do not need a man to complete my life because it is full of love and contentment, and what Michael does with his life has no bearing on mine now. I have long ago chosen a different path and resolve to put the past behind me and go forth unafraid. Forgive me, dear friend, if that sounds like another one of my Irish declarations. Thank you once again for your genuine interest and caring.

Your friend,
Catherine

Great is life .. and real and mystical ... wherever and whoever,
Great is death. .... Sure as life holds all parts together, death holds all parts together;
Sure as the stars return again after they merge in the light, death is great as life.

"Great is Life"
Leaves of Grass
Walt Whitman

Chapter Eight
1867–1869

Letter from Delphina, in French

Paris
Île de France
France
10 January 1867

Dear Madame,
   Please forgive me for not answering more of your letters. I forgot most of my English and was too embarrassed to disappoint your high expectations of me. I am twenty years old, and I am married now. He is rich and from a fancy family. My parents arranged the marriage without asking me.
   I miss speaking English and living in New York. Being there with you is among my happiest memories. I recall how much I loved being taught by you. Reading with you each night as I fell asleep is a distant dream. You were the only person I ever knew who thought I was smart. Everyone said I was pretty, but only you expected me to read and write well.
   I learned about why we left. It was the Panic of 1857. My father's bank did not receive their gold shipment when the ship *Central America* sank. Even when we got to France, the Panic was there, too. They said it reached the entire world.

Ah, Madame, you know how we always loved weddings. Mine was so beautiful. My dress was the finest Chantilly lace, with a train that flowed down the long aisle. Flowers filled the whole church, and *le tout Paris* came to see me. My husband was so dashing and handsome in his morning suit. His name is Alphonse, and he is an ambassador's son studying to be a lawyer. Now I am a wife, whatever that means. They tell me I am not a very good one, as I cannot seem to live up to what is expected of me.

I pray you remember and think about me. On my wedding day, I missed you most of all. You are on the other side of the world but will always be my proper mother, Madame. Until we are together again, *a bientôt*.

With love,
Delphina

Letter from Catherine, in French

129 Cedar Street
New York City
March 9, 1867

Dear Delphina,

Of course, I could never forget my girl. I think about you almost every day. What joyous news to hear about your nuptials and the beautiful bride you were. You will make a wonderful wife because you have so much love to give. In their wisdom, your parents have matched you with a capable young man. Promise me you will try to consider him in a sympathetic light, especially when things are difficult. Like you, he is trying his best, something easy to forget. It is a lesson some of us recognize late and still struggle with.

Sometimes our best effort falls short, but especially then, we can forgive and forget and go forward despite it. I am enclosing a little pink dress you used to wear that I pilfered out of the ragbag years ago. You are wearing it in the daguerreotype I have of you. Just as my young "daughter" wore it, I kept it so your daughter may wear it someday. I missed you on your wedding day. If love has wings to fly, I was there, dear one, then, now, and always.

Your loving
Madame

Letter from Patrick, under the door

129 Cedar Street
New York City
December 14, 1867

Dear Catherine,

No longer can we chat on the stairs in the building and keep one another abreast of our lives. My recent illness never left me, as Julia stands guard at my bedside. The illness has taken a sudden turn for the worse, and my time is swiftly coming to an end. The previous bout of scarlet fever has left me with a worsening case of rheumatic fever. After being given a second chance at fatherhood, my only regret is not being able to raise little Jay. Look after him if you can. He is far too young to lose a father.

I missed being your husband in this life, but we will meet in another. That is what the people in Nicaragua said years ago. We did not miss being friends on paper, but I regret that we never freely engaged in person. You deserved better, my dear one. A part of me that I gave to no one else will remain with you. Farewell, my Catherine.

Your forever penfriend,
Patrick

SUSAN MCGUIRK

Letter from Catherine, under the door

129 Cedar Street
New York City
February 3, 1868

Dear Patrick,

With Julia hovering at your doorstep, I waited for an unguarded moment to slip this letter to you. I miss the days when I could leave a letter in your hallway box when walking about was still possible for you. How ironic that I am missing you just as my apparition of a husband has become manifest. What a testament to your character and friendship that his long-awaited contact seems less than monumental, given your suffering.

How could I know that the stranger on the *Queen Victoria* in another lifetime would mean so much in this one? You taught me to examine my choices, forget regret, and accept fate.

You also taught me that love comes to those who wait. Your beautiful and stalwart Julia proves it so. Thank you for listening to my problems all these years and never losing faith in me, Patrick.

I long to go to your bedside, but our friendship has lived by the pen. Now it will die by one due to your frailty and your family's need for privacy. As you described the Nicaraguan people's beliefs, I do believe there is more. We will forever share our lives in the hereafter. I will cherish and keep each precious missive from you. Farewell, dear friend, until we walk together in the gloaming.

Your forever penfriend,
Catherine

Letter from Catherine

129 Cedar Street
New York City
November 21, 1868

Dear Cousin Jack,
    Welcome to New York, and I wish you good luck in your new prac-

tice as a doctor. I heard you enjoyed a reunion with Johnny in Bridgehampton before setting up your office. After your years together growing up in Ireland, he will always consider you more of a brother than a cousin. Your dear father, Bryan, would be proud of his son and nephew.

I am writing because I have not felt well for a while. I would like to visit your office, which is within walking distance for me, for an examination. Luckily, my legs are still strong enough. I will be there the day after tomorrow when I am at liberty from my teaching. Thank you.

Your cousin,
Catherine

Letter from Doctor Jack

154 Ninth Avenue
New York, New York
December 19, 1868

Dear Cousin Catherine,

With a heavy heart, I must tell you that the ailment you suffer from is consumption. It is a wasting disease of the lungs, but it may progress slowly enough to give you more time. While this is terrible news, I pledge to be by your side with all the medical knowledge I possess. You supported and encouraged me in medical school in Scotland. Without your financial support for my tuition, I would never have graduated.

There is no effective treatment for consumption, but I promise to make you as comfortable as possible. What I lack in experience will be more than compensated for by my devotion to your care. Growing up with Cousin Johnny after the rest of you emigrated made me closer to your whole family. I will not let you down.

Your cousin,
Doctor Jack

SUSAN MCGUIRK

Letter from Catherine

129 Cedar Street
New York City
January 9, 1869

Dear Jane,

    I am on my way to somewhere I have not been before. Consumption lives within me. Though increasingly challenging, I can still conceal the illness from those around me. However, I cannot deny that I am at the crossroads of a fading life. In a brief time, I must admit my situation to my employers. I have symptoms of increasing fatigue and coughing. Other stirrings linger beyond my intentional thoughts that are new to me.

    A rush of air on my cheek calls to mind the fluttering of a picture book's pages being quickly thumbed through. Fading sounds just out of reach lend an ear to whispers of a tiny voice in the night. A rustling behind me hints at a hovering bird over my shoulder. As I fold my fingers around my pendant of Erca, I whisper to your spirits, "Not yet. Not when there is so much to put right while I still have the chance."

Your friend,
Catherine

Letter from Jane

Liberty Street
Eastville
Sag Harbor, New York
February 7, 1869

Dear Catherine,

    Putting things right is what we all try to do. I have a house. It puts to right that my father had to walk off Indian Fields settlement so we would not starve. I purchased the headstone for Silas. It made our painful parting right again. My house is fully paid for, but I still have money in the Sag Harbor Savings Bank. It puts to right all the serving of

Mr. Mulford and the laundry I took in. I live alone in my home with my parlor shelves filled with my collections. I have put my life to right.

You will also put things to right, Catherine. You have time, and now you understand. I told you something a long time ago: "Go forth unafraid."

Your friend,
Jane

Letter from Ellen, in English

Indiana County
Blairsville, Pennsylvania
February 9, 1869

Dear Cath,

May this letter arrive before you see Michael's newest advertisement in the Missing Friends notices. Rather than celebrating my first letter to you in English, I dread it. I left out important information when I told you about his new family in Ohio. Michael also has a daughter of his own, born to his now-late wife, a little girl named Mary. I was wrong to tell you so late, but I wanted to spare you too many shocks at the same time. Also, I did not want to ruin your chance of ever writing to him. It was selfish, and it only made things worse.

Michael told me this important information: "I placed the second advertisement because I hold proceeds from the sale of grazing land bought in 1848 at the Old Farm near Sag Harbor. I have saved it for Cathy for years. Even if she refuses it, maybe she could at least designate an heir who could accept the bequest." Now that he knows you are alive, he asked, "Would you ask Cathy if I can send the $2,200 to her?" Even if you want to throw it away, Cath, you could do some good with this money. I also still have the letter from the battlefield that Michael wrote to you. I will wait for permission to send it.

Your almost sister,
Ellen

Letter from Catherine, in English

129 Cedar Street
New York City
March 7, 1869

Dear Ellen,
How could you possibly know that Michael having a child of his own is stabbing me through the heart? It is because I never disclosed something significant to you. I lost a baby a few months after Michael left. I should have shared this vital information with you, and I realize now it was wrong of me.

The future seems filled with the same dilemmas as the past. For the third time, a Missing Friends notice has interrupted a period of welcome routine. Long ago, I stopped reading the newspaper where the advertisements appeared. Unfortunately, my employer, Mr. Bose, spotted the advertisement in his newspaper and pointed it out.

MISSING FRIENDS

*OF CATHERINE MCGUIRK, who lived in Sag Harbor, Long Island, in 1844 and 1845; when last heard of she was in Greenport. Any information of her will
Be thankfully received by Michael Heffernan, Smithville Post-office, Wayne county, Ohio.*

These dispatches are haunting me like ghosts. No matter how hard I run, I cannot escape them, while my resolve and intentions have no effect. It feels as though Michael is purposely provoking me, even if it is not his intention. He may mean it as a gesture of kindness, but these repeated notices must stop. I do not want Michael's pity or help at this late juncture.

The time I have left on this earth should not be spent in turmoil over him. You see, Ellen, I am ill with consumption. I crave peace, but it is out of my reach. Yet none of this is your fault. Once again, my sister, acting as messenger has put you in the line of fire. Once again, I apologize. Despite everything, I am so proud of your letter in English. Congratulations.

Your sister,
Cath

Letter from Catherine

Saint Peter's Church
Barclay Street
New York City
March 8, 1869

Dear Pierre,
   Now that you are in heaven, you must have fulfilled the French origin of your name and become an actual saint. I am writing to you from our church today to capture a hint of your former serenity. On the wall above your old pew is an oil painting of a woman, with the name "Elizabeth Seton" at the bottom of the frame. A memory returns of you saying, "I tried to model my acts of charity after Elizabeth." I cling to the recollection, hoping for more.
   Pierre, despair wells up inside me, and I hate these feelings. Even I recognize Frank's warning of vindictiveness and realize I am guilty. My challenge to rise above has fallen flat. Yet I have tried to live a life of purpose and dignity. It seems Michael is robbing me of what little peace I have in the time left to me.
   I hear your voice again: "Elizabeth Seton was a woman who lost her husband and two children and died young herself. The cause was consumption, the terrible illness my sister and stepdaughter died from."
   There is no Bell of Saint Colmcille to drink from that would have saved any of us from this disease. Pierre, you once told me, "Elizabeth died at just forty-six years old." That is barely more than my age of forty-four. It makes me feel less alone that Elizabeth shared my condition. "She founded the first charitable institution in New York City, the

Society for the Relief of Poor Widows with Small Children." You told me that on our last day together.

As my distress fades, I can almost sense you are here with me. My shallow breathing is slowing, and I can fill my ailing lungs more deeply than I have for days. I entered the church feeling upset, but the reverie calms me. As I stand up, a sense of purpose presses me forward. Time is my enemy, but my life is not over.

The sadness and bitterness inside me are receding. I feel lighter and stronger than when I entered the church. An image of a gentle, conflicted young man with faraway eyes appears in my thoughts. A glimmer of gratitude and relief hovers. Could this be what forgiveness feels like, Pierre? My hand closes over the ring on my finger. What a relief not to have crushed it on the sidewalk. I finally understand your lesson of mercy, Pierre. These words are in your honor: I vow at last to write to the husband I have been married to for over twenty years.

Your friend,
Catherine

Letter from Catherine

129 Cedar Street
New York City
March 9, 1869

Dear Jane,

Returning home from St. Peter's yesterday, I passed a carriage with the sound of content gurgling. I saw a baby with platinum curls that matched the hue of the hair in the locket inside my hope chest. Once home, I went to find it, which proved challenging after five years unseen. Inside it, next to the locket of hair was the still sealed, yellowed letter from Michael, dated 1856, over ten years earlier. The time you spoke of long ago has come. I tore it open and began reading the plaintive wails of a lost seaman.

Jane, I made so many empty promises to change. I hid behind anger and used it as an excuse to avoid examining my faults. I am tired of being myself.

Your friend,
Catherine

❦

Letter from Michael

Faial, Azores
December 17, 1856

Dear Cathy,

    I could see the masts of the *Bark Neva* against the sky as I searched Greenport for you. They followed me up and down the streets, provoking me each time I encountered another blind alley. The lads in the tavern said the *Neva* was looking for a crew. I tried to duck the sight of the vessel while looking for you. The tall masts jutted behind every landmark I passed. The dead ends accrued as the possibilities of finding you shrank daily. Finally, my feet steered me up the gangway. I boarded the vessel and spoke to Captain Conklin about signing on.

    It was so familiar and right. What a fool I was ever to doubt this is where I belong. Though I was never the reader you were, I eventually read the seaman's bible, *Moby-Dick; or, The Whale*, like a good whaler. Your old friend Melville could explain our plight better than anyone: "As for me, I am tormented with an everlasting itch for things remote. I love to sail forbidden seas, and land on barbarous coasts." It was not until we were halfway to the Azores Islands that panic overtook me. By then, it was far too late.

    I have done it again. When the next step eludes me, and my head feels like it will burst from frustration, I run. I ran to the sea, the gold rush, and away from the one chance I had to find you. I should have stayed in Greenport and secured some labor. Undoubtedly, a hint of you would have emerged if I had just bided my time. What truly galls me is that I walked right into a trap. I went back on my promise to you and did as your brothers predicted, becoming a whaleman again.

    My misery is almost unendurable. If you were alive and waiting somewhere for me, your presence on earth would be manifest in some way. I feel nothing. I am living in this hell of stench, blood, and oil from carcasses with no escape. No one owns the sea, but the opposite can be all too true.

That I ever thought of this life as freedom was a delusion. I could accuse Melville of perpetrating it, but I needed no help to believe. It was always a way to punish myself, for what I cannot say. Maybe it was for reaching for the North Star of home, feminine warmth, beauty, and comfort. They are so far beyond my grasp that I cannot believe I ever possessed such a dream. Would God smite me with this much contrition if you were among the living?

Your loving husband,
Michael

Letter from Catherine

129 Cedar Street
New York City
March 27, 1869

Dear Ellen,

It took far too long for me to appreciate this, but I would not have survived without your unquestioning help, support, faith, and love. I took these gestures from you for granted, as though they were my due when they were outright gifts from your bountiful and generous heart. I came between you and your brother and then asked you to betray your blood for my sake. It was so unfair to you, and not only did you not punish me for this low sin, but you stayed loyally by my side.

I did not deserve your sisterhood, but always cherished it. Putting myself before you is something I will always regret. I was so blessed to have you in my life. If I could go back, I would throw my arms around you daily, kiss your cheek, and say, "I love you." Dear Ellen, let us part on these words as none more need to be spoken. Your warm smile shines on me still.

Your sister,
Cath

Letter from Mamie

Hayground
Corwith Farm
Bridgehampton, New York
March 29, 1869

Dear Aunt Cath,

    Thanks to you, I am now officially engaged to William Tyndall. It would not have been possible to appease his family without plans for a proper wedding. Presbyterians appear more formal about social niceties than our folk. Because you have graciously offered to provide for our nuptials, they now seem to grudgingly accept a Catholic "war orphan" as their daughter-in-law.

    I love William so much, and losing him would have broken my heart. You rescued me, Auntie. Yes, Pa would probably not approve of me marrying a Protestant, and certainly not in a Presbyterian Church, even though his two dear friends who sponsored his citizenship were Presbyterians. Times change, and two Fee girls are also engaged to Protestants. I guess young people either do not remember the past feuds or never knew they existed. When I did not have one, you acted as my mother, and now I will be respectable in a beautiful dress with all my family around me to celebrate.

    I will wear the cameo pendant of Erca you gave me when I walk down the aisle. That you bequeathed it to me in honor of my mother means so much. Thank you for explaining that it symbolizes that motherhood is eternal, which you said she helped teach you. I never imagined Mama in the role of teacher, especially to one as cultured as you. It is so special that you shared that knowledge with her and passed it on to me in the pendant. When I have a daughter, I promise to do the same.

It is a surprise that you shared a bond, as no one ever speaks of her. By telling me of your time together, you have returned a part of her to me. I hope the deeper tie to Mama that you provided will help me become a better wife and future mother. I will think about you each time I wear the pendant and will cherish it always. Get well soon, dear Auntie.

Your grateful niece,
Mamie

Letter from Jane

Liberty Street,
Eastville
Sag Harbor, New York
March 31, 1869

Dear Catherine,

The end of our time is coming, so I must speak my mind. For so long, you could not forgive your man. Now you have. I hope it lifts the hardness you have carried in your heart since you were a young woman. You have toted a heavier weight for just as long.

Frank told you that your view of Michael was unkind, but you judged yourself more bitterly. You need to lay your burden down, and it is not too late. You can begin again, even if your life is almost over. Every day has meaning. You can spend the last few by putting things to right.

Maybe you were stubborn and harbored ill will longer than need be, but there were so many good things you did. I know the Irish are close to the land, just as my people are. Yet, Catherine, you are a woman of the mind, not the earth. Your teaching was righteous and important. You helped your family and lived a good life. You learned some ways of my people, which always pleased me. Even though we are from different traditions, we are alike in our natures.

Now is the time for you to forgive the person you have treated the most harshly, Catherine. The time has come for you to forgive yourself.

Your friend,
Jane

DEAR MISSING FRIEND

Letter from Catherine

129 Cedar Street
New York City
April 21, 1869

Dear Jane,

Today, your spirits gave me the strength to write to you for probably the last time. My dear teacher, you saved your best lesson for last. I thought it would be difficult to forgive Michael, but the burden I carried simply dissolved into dust. It was suddenly hard to summon, as though it never existed. That was never the outcome I anticipated. Despite my weakness, being released from guilt makes me feel almost girlish and giddy. How liberating it can be when remorse and regret fly away.

When I was a young woman aboard the *Queen Victoria*, I promised this to myself: Someday, I will not be told what to do. I always wondered, *What would it be like to do anything I wanted, whenever I wanted?* I look out the window at the birds flying high. At this moment, this is exactly and only what I wish to be doing. In despair, I once said, "My ambitions are to laugh, to run, to feel, to love again." Well, maybe I cannot run, but looking out this window, my heart laughs and loves again.

Thank you for listening in all my times of need, Jane. After I left Sag Harbor, I missed you, but it was not our destiny to spend the years together. Still, I felt you with me and still relied on you. You once told me, "We are tied to one another by experience, pain, sorrow, and trust." However, you left out the most essential element that ties us. I love you, Jane, and will miss you always. Look for me flying above.

Your friend,
Catherine

Myself moving forward then and now and forever,
Gathering and showing more always and with velocity,
Infinite and omnigenous, and the like of these among them,
Not too exclusive toward the reachers of my remembrancers,
Picking out here one that I love, and now go with him on brotherly terms.

"Song of Myself," 32
Leaves of Grass
Walt Whitman

Chapter Nine

1869

Letter from Catherine

129 Cedar Street
New York City
April 2, 1869

Dear Michael,

    I am writing this letter for both of us. It is never to be sent but has a specific goal. It is not to revisit old vendettas but to banish them forever. If I vent my harsh, cold, and unforgiving feelings one last time, they will be forever dead and buried. Then we can both be at peace. Though I am the sole recipient of this rant, it will absolve you as well.

    If only you had never tried to find me and stayed gone. I can never stop loving or hating you like a curse. I hate you because I am elated you are still alive, though you are like a ghost haunting me from the lost world. I hate you for the hole in my heart and for returning to fill it. I hate you for trapping me when I was offered a way out.

    Perhaps I fought to keep us apart to punish you or myself. I found strength, but at a steep price. Instead of a spouse, I learned to live with loneliness, my constant companion.

    The lesson I learned from you was that the only person I could depend upon in this life was myself. There was no path out of our marriage, with death the only release. A lifelong oath meant another promise of true love was impossible. You remained my husband these past twenty-two years in name only, not flesh.

Your wife,
Cathy

Letter from Catherine

129 Cedar Street
New York City
April 23, 1869

Dear Michael,

I finally read the letter you wrote me from the *Bark Neva*. I am sorry it took over ten years to read it. My many mistakes are clear to me now. I walked through aspects of my adult life blind, denying what I knew to be true. I could not or would not open my eyes. Only God can forgive me for hiding from the light of truth. For this, I am truly sorry.

I regret the loss you will experience when you read this. We both feel the sorrow of so many years gone with no resolution. We lost a child the year you left, a daughter with your eyes. She lived only a few hours, and I could not bear to give her a name. I am sorry to disclose this sad news in such a stark way. At this very late juncture, I offer you my sincere condolences.

Another piece of dreadful news is that I am dying of consumption. Again, I apologize for the abruptness. It seems there is no graceful way to reveal such information. I believe you thought I was dead when you married the widow. I commend you for your war service, and I hope you are happy. Thank you for the proceeds from the land. Among other things, Tor's son Francis can now make a deposit on a blacksmith shop in Brooklyn.

I failed to write to you for survival, not spite. You were my love, and you disappeared. I became a different person, a woman a long-ago young couple would not recognize. I was not very strong and certainly not tough, but I found my way. Your ring is still on my finger, which has done what it promised. It has promoted forgiveness. There are no regrets. We are released. Redemption is upon us.

Your wife,
Cathy

Letter from Michael

Pittsburgh Avenue
Wooster, Ohio
May 15, 1869

Dear Cathy,

    I did everything I could think of. When I came back looking, there was no sign of you. I only went to Ohio when I truly believed you were gone. This is not to blame you. If I had the chance to do it again, I hope I would not have boarded those vessels. We both know that it would not be true.

    I could not stop myself. It was a chance to escape plowing and sail to freedom. I denied it would take years away when all facts pointed to the contrary. After the *Neva* voyage, I finally did reach the elusive Arctic after the captain's empty threat to sail there on the last voyage before we married. Our vessel was among the first to sail that far. Reaching the top of the globe was otherworldly, and the confectionery cliffs encased in mist were dreamlike. With the preternatural quiet and frozen stillness, the setting seemed almost sacred, like the closest place to heaven on earth. We ultimately reached a place where the whales were plentiful. Seeing them feeding and diving so freely with their young in that celestial paradise, I understood that I could never kill another whale. I left the vessel at the next stop in Barrow, Alaska.

    This is selfish and cruel of me, but I never stopped missing you during my years of family life. I survived not just the Battle of Atlanta, but Bull Run and Gettysburg, by picturing your face. I wanted to be still. Why was I compelled to charge headlong to the end of the world?

Unlike most men, I actually reached it but found nothing. Then I doubled back and crossed the world again, with my hands still empty. When I got to Ohio to stake the claim, I felt like an old man, tired and spent.

Since I left you, I have seen the worst a man could see. Armageddon on the battlefield, mining desperadoes starving in filthy camps, pristine island women desecrated by craven sailors, and saloons full of thieving varmints. I lost all hope. Then I would remember that you might be somewhere in the world.

A small part of me knew that boarding the last ship in Greenport would mean exile from you forever. Nonetheless I always believed I would see you again. I will never recover from the fact that you slipped from my grasp for good.

I worried I would never accomplish bequeathing you the money from the sale of the land in Sag Harbor. It was the only chance to make my mistakes less awful. Now I am an older man with enough means but still no way to help you. You never made it easy, Cathy. People make mistakes. I am so sorry for your loss, for our loss. Thank you for caring for my sister all those years, another of my failings. You must know it was always you, Cathy.

All my love,
Michael

Letter from Ellen, in English, left on the bedside table

129 Cedar Street
New York City
May 18, 1869

Dear Cath,

How fortunate that my in-laws called me to the building in time to see you once more. Thank you for agreeing to my company even though I broke the doctor's No Visitors order. I should have written ahead that I was staying with my relatives, but I was afraid you would refuse to see me.

The letters in a pile beside your bed worried me, as I assumed you were too tired to read them all. Thank you for taking my recommendation to record passages from each into one letter. It is not an ideal solution, but it is better than the letters left unread in your weakened state.

I am happy that the years of English lessons with you and Papa Burke helped me complete such an important task. Now you can read your loved ones' special thoughts whenever you are strong enough.

Your brother Tor wrote:

We have come a long way from home. It was another life when we stood together under a starry Erin sky. I still miss the singing, dancing, and dreaming of our long-lost home. I am sorry you had such a twisted path to follow. You deserved better. Until we meet again, I will always miss you.

Johnny wrote:

I will never stop missing my big sis, now and forever. Kiss Mam, Da, and Frank for me.

Susie wrote:

You are my best friend and the girl of my heart. On this side of the ocean, we have shared the same family, name, and adult lives. On the other side of the sea, we shared our girlhoods, hopes, and the hill we ran down together. For the first time, you are outrunning me but look over your shoulder for me to catch up.

Finally, here is what your friend Jane wrote:

I will look at your gift of the statue of Saint Francis holding the birds and always think of you. Your faith's tradition of this holy man is very curious, as are the words on the bottom: *Does not my father feed the birds of the sky?* I will turn this small vision over in my mind. Fly away home, my friend. I will look for you soaring above.

Cath, you are my sister, the only one I have. We were a pair that stood the test of time. Michael brought us together, but never kept us apart. You always surprised me. Forgive me one last surprise as I leave the letter Michael wrote you from the battlefield in your hope chest. To think I might have missed going to New York with you. I will stay by your side as long as you will have me.

Your forever sister,
Ellen

Letter from Michael

Peachtree Creek
Atlanta, Georgia
July 18, 1864

Dear Cathy,

I am crouching in a trench beside a stream by the name of Peachtree Creek, deep in enemy territory, just before dawn. I have a wet, dirty piece of paper I have been saving in a pocket. There is a broken pencil stub to write with. When daylight comes, we will attack. To get here, we crossed the Chattahoochee River, which was supposed to be the last barrier to Atlanta. Now my unit must cross a deep line of Confederates to reach there.

After too many battles in too many states for the previous two years, hope has deserted me. This existence is somewhere between living and dying, and the latter seems preferable. Death keeps whispering in my ear, luring me closer like a mother's embrace, knowing I have no resistance left. If anything, I welcome the release.

Yesterday, it almost came. I was standing next to a caisson carriage of gunpowder that was hit by an enemy shell. The explosion blew me into the sky. I felt my body slow in mid-air. Seconds seemed like minutes as the moments of my life whirled by like a spinning top. I was in a place you told me about, one that you have been to – somewhere on the other side. I called out to you, "Cathy," but you did not answer. When I heard nothing, it confirmed to me that you were still on the living side of the divide I had crossed.

I hit the ground with a violent blow. When I eventually opened my eyes, all was dark, and I thought I was dead. I might as well have been in hell because I was lying in a sea of dead bodies. It took a long time to determine where I was and why I was there.

I stood and tried to make my way back to my regiment in the

twilight. I heard the creek gurgling out of one ear and followed it until I came to a camp. At first, I could not tell whether it was Yankee or Rebel. In the first light, I saw our flag flying over a tent. I fell to my knees and cried.

Now you are all I think about. You make me put one foot before the other when I long to lie down and surrender to my battered body. I will lay my head on the opposite side of my now-deaf ear, and the silence will lull me. I will find you. I must so I can stay alive. I promise myself that if I am spared, I will find you.

Love,
Michael

Letter from Catherine

129 Cedar Street
New York City
May 21, 1869

Dear Michael,
Today, I read the letter you wrote me from the Battle of Atlanta in 1864 for the first time. It was in my hope chest, next to me, to remind me Mam is not far. It was so moving, Michael. There was always something of the poet in you.

I am sorry to falter. There is not enough left in me to respond. As much as I convinced myself that my heart was hardened, it never was. I am still your wife. Though I had a chance, I never gave myself to anyone else because I pledged myself to you. This poem from Walt Whitman is all I have left to give: "I am not to speak to you, I am to think of you when I sit alone or wake at night alone, I am to wait, I do not doubt I am to meet you again, I am to see to it that I do not lose you."

Your loving wife,
Cathy

SUSAN MCGUIRK

Letter from Michael

Pittsburgh Avenue
Wooster, Ohio
June 12, 1869

Dear Cathy,
    I hope you got my reply to your letter as I am still waiting to hear from you. Maybe you will already be gone when this arrives. It has always been too late for us, and it is too late now. I will see you again. It will not be here, but somewhere else far away. I will come and find you there, wherever it is. We will never miss each other again. We will finally be together on the other side.

All my love,
Michael

I swear I see now that every thing without exception has an eternal soul!
The trees have, rooted in the ground! the weeds of the sea have!
the animals!
I swear I think there is nothing but immortality!

"To Think of Time," 11
Leaves of Grass
Walt Whitman

Epilogue
1870

Letter from Francis

Tomasina Farm
Scuttle Hole Road
Bridgehampton, New York
June 18, 1870

Dear Aunt Cath,
   Never in my life has something so miraculous happened. I know you always thought about me, even with so much time gone by since I last saw you. My mother said it was because I was the closest to a son you ever had. Now I feel like your son because you always understood how vital my trade is to me. My ambition will be fulfilled because you left me a down payment on a blacksmith shop.
   The gift you bequeathed me is more precious than the financial inheritance. I will cherish the letter you sent with them all my life:

   Dear Francis,
   Enclosed is a familial gift that is not ultimately for you but will be your responsibility. As the future patriarch of the family, please safeguard it for your future wife. My wedding ring is hers to keep.
   The ring has traveled the world. It lived in a pocket on the high seas for over a year and visited many countries and several continents. It was

made in Portugal of chrysoberyl, a precious mineral found there. Chrysoberyl is said to help someone see both sides of a situation and to aid with compassion, generosity, and forgiveness. Of the three, the greatest is forgiveness, of which we can never have too much.

As the Irish say, until we meet again, dear Francis.

Your loving Aunt,
Catherine

You are the only person who has talked to me about my namesake, Uncle Frank, without looking away. Pa and Ma always felt sorrowful that he left Mamie alone. "You have the honor of being named for a great man, brave and patriotic enough to die for his country and liberty." You wrote me those words when I was still a boy. When I first read them, I felt proud to be his nephew and bear his name. I still do. I know you will never get this letter. My love to you, Auntie.

Your favorite nephew,
Francis

Letter from Tor

Tomasina Farm
Scuttle Hole Road
Bridgehampton, New York
June 20, 1870

Dear Michael,
It fell to me as the next of kin to gather the belongings of your wife. Her letters were the most abundant of Cath's meager possessions, more than her books. I was unsure where or to whom they should go, so I am sending them to you. I did not read them, as it did not seem my right to do so.

She wrote this request: "Please divide my books between Jane Perdue and my nieces and nephews. I left one book for Michael, James Fenimore Cooper's *The Pathfinder*. I kindly request you send it to him with the proviso he still needs to finish it. There is an envelope in the book's pages addressed to me. Please do not let it fall out of the book." Even in the end, Cath was always the teacher.

Any man would commend you on your exemplary war record. I can only imagine what Bull Run and Gettysburg cost you in terms of horror and suffering. My younger brother was at Gettysburg and cannot even speak of it. It is regrettable that you lost much of your hearing in the Battle of Atlanta.

I am giving you these letters so I can let Cath go. It is hard to know if they will spur you on or hinder your progress. You forfeited marriage to my sister, but it still seems fitting that you are the next of kin, not me.

I am older now, as we all are, and see that human beings are complicated creatures. They can no longer be easily sorted, like when I was younger. We all try our best and fail but continue. That is what I am doing now. I judged you early on without knowing you, and I apologize for that.

The irony is that we have something in common after seeming so different. We both became independent farmers and made good in America as Irishmen. The only lesson I ever understood was to buy some land and work it to undo the past. After traveling so many other routes, you settled on the same destination.

We also both loved my sister. It pains me that if I had gotten along with you better, Cath might have suffered less. My greatest regret is not spending more time with her. This last letter from a bank should be added to the collected letters I leave to you.

Your brother-in-law,
Tor

*

Letter from the Manager of the Emigrant Savings of New York

49 Chambers Street
New York City
July 3, 1870

Dear Mr. McGuirk,

I am the manager of the Emigrant Savings Bank in New York. This letter is to inform you that Catherine M. Heffernan made several bequests from the proceeds of her bank account. Mrs. Heffernan made this request: "Please split the final amount left in the account among my nieces and nephews. My nephew Francis already has a separate bequest for a real estate deposit."

Beyond the familial inheritances, per your sister's wishes, three additional bequests will be taken from the account. They are for Saint David A.M.E. Zion Church in Sag Harbor and Saint Peter's Church on Barclay Street. A child named John "Jay" Lynch of the same address as Mrs. Heffernan's last is the final bequest.

In the fifteen years she had the account, Mrs. Heffernan made many deposits, with limited withdrawals. This is not the usual practice, so the final amount was substantial, enabling each recipient to receive a generous gift. Please find the paperwork enclosed. The bank offers condolences to your family on the loss of our gracious and loyal customer, Catherine M. Heffernan.

Yours truly,
Stephen Hurley

Letter from Michael

Pittsburgh Avenue
Wooster, Ohio
August 5, 1870

Dear Tor,

Thank you for the letters. You are correct that they will have the intended effect, as they immediately became my most prized possessions. I agree that we have traits in common. You said, "My greatest regret is not spending more time with her." I feel the same. As many nights as that kept me up, part of me understood that Cathy was not like either of us. Now that I have read the letters, my eyes are finally open.

Cathy lived a life of the mind. She could survive almost anywhere if she had her beloved books and willing pupils. Her physical circumstances being reduced between the two positions did not matter to her. She only cared that the children wanted to learn and to be loved. Now I understand that the love they returned sustained Cathy. My only comfort in my ongoing self-reproach is that she chose the life she led. At least she never slipped through your fingers.

Your brother-in-law,
Michael

Letter from Tor

Tomasina Farm
Scuttle Hole Road
Bridgehampton, New York
September 12, 1870

Dear Michael,
    Please be at peace that, as human beings, we are at the mercy of the tides of fortune. Fate deals us the only hand we must play.
    I give you much credit for the inheritance you gave Cath. The total of it was worth almost my entire farm. It made her happy and at peace to use it to help her family. My son was one recipient. Francis reminds me of you as a young man. He has that same otherworldly look in his eyes, and we are at constant loggerheads. The problem could be my failure to understand people who differ from me.
    Francis's future as a blacksmith would not have been possible without the funds you provided. With his wavering temperament and stubborn mentality, he sorely needed direction and a chance, which you provided. Please consider how you rescued my son during your next bout of remorse.
    My young nephew, Doctor Jack, only thirty years old, suffered from consumption like his patient Cath. He came to the farm so he would not die alone. When the priest came to administer the Last Rites, he said, "Since I am far from my da, I am praying to his namesake and forebear, Bryan. He was a priest who died a martyr in prison for the crime of tending to his flock." I like to think both Cath and Bryan were there to welcome Jack to heaven. None of us know what the future has in store. We all must follow my sister's example and love while we can.

Your brother-in-law,
Tor

SUSAN MCGUIRK

Letter from Michael

Pittsburgh Avenue
Wooster, Ohio
October 12, 1870

Dear Tor,
    I am sorry about Doctor Jack. What a great sorrow for such a promising young man to be stricken. The previous letters you wrote have given me much of importance to consider. I spent so much of my life thinking there was time. I ran from my sole provider of happiness, Cathy, to the farthest places I could find. The closest I came to peace was finally becoming a father at age thirty-six. It provides me with what no sea, whale, mine, shipyard, or battlefield ever did.
    I found one last letter in the pages of the book Cathy asked you to send to me. I never did finish *The Pathfinder*. Long ago, Joe Josey wrote asking your sister to come to my aid. Cathy wrote a note on the bottom of Joe's letter to me dated the day before she died. She must have known the letter's journey was not quite complete.

Your brother-in-law,
Michael

༄

Letter from Joe Josey

Hawaii, Sandwich Islands
December 29, 1856

Dear Mrs. Heffernan,
    We only met once, but I have a bond with you. My name is Joe Josey. I helped pick out a wedding ring for you when your husband was at my home in the Azores Islands years ago. I served as a seaman on the bark, *Byron*. Our vessel had a gam in the South Pacific with the bark, *Neva*, which Michael was serving on.
    I found him unwell and thought someone in his family should know. Michael did not take my advice: "You have a malady, whatever it may be. The wise course would be to leave the bark, *Neva*'s employ and book a passage home."

I cannot say what was wrong with him, but I never knew him to be so distant. He said little and looked away when we talked. He did not say a friendly hello and spoke in a flat voice. Besides his strange way, his physical health seemed fine, though he looked pale and thin.

Our vessel left Hawaii to return to New York. Michael asked me to give a book called *The Pathfinder* to my crewmate, Charles Fee. He was to give it to his sister Susie to hold for you. I stuck my letter inside the book so it could find a path to you.

Yours truly,
Joe Josey

This book voyaged from me to you, to Joe, to Charles (the letter within), to Susie, to Frank, to Johnny, returning to me. May it find its way to you once more. Had I allowed the letter it held to cross my path, I would have crossed yours.

Forgive me.

THE END

Author's Note

While conducting some family research several years ago, I ran across the actual advertisement the whaler Michael Heffernan placed in the Missing Friends syndicated newspaper column for lost Irish people. It was 1864, and he was looking for his wife, Catherine, my second great-aunt, in Sag Harbor from a location in Ohio. It was intriguing to imagine how they had lost each other. A second advertisement surfaced that Michael placed four years later, still trying to locate his wife. I was surprised to realize that Catherine never answered her husband's first query. Why did she refuse to answer him? My imagination was sparked, and from there this story was born.

Although my depictions of Catherine and her family and friends in this novel are based on real people, they are fictionalized in terms of their motivations and feelings. I tracked their movements and whereabouts to flesh out the story, and the plot unfolds according to the records of the characters' lives. That there were instances of documentation that matched my invented motivations is a coincidence. It was difficult to fit timelines precisely, and there were instances of stretching dates to meet events.

When the action takes place on Long Island, the records are more reliable as there were fewer examples of people with the same name. In New York City, there were multiple individuals with the same names and similar locations. Choices were made that ruled out the development of other potential characters, who remained unexplored. Circumstantial evidence helped with these decisions.

AUTHOR'S NOTE

The sources that illustrated my characters' journeys were varied. Whaling logs to ship manifests and passenger lists for crossing the Atlantic and the world were located. There are federal and state census records showing addresses and information like family members, occupations, nationality, net worth, acreage and what crops were grown. Maps help situate characters, while bank and employment records demonstrate quotidian lives. Birth, death, marriage, war and newspaper records, as well as burial locations, show the passages of each character's lives. Extensive reading informed my research, and there is a bibliography of sixty references, including books and dissertations, on my website, www.susanmcguirk.com.

I also visited the ancestral townland, Mullinclavin, in Ireland that Cath came from. A local historian, Larry McDermott, showed me the actual McGuirk farm and the proverbial hill she and her best friend ran down. At the bottom was a town called Kingscourt, the location of Cabra Castle, where they worked the harvest to save money for their passages, and the Irish Society School where Cath learned the English and French languages.

In Termonmaguirk, County Tyrone, Northern Ireland, I was hosted by Nuala McGurk, a teacher at Dean Maguirc College, named for our martyred priest ancestor, Bryan. She showed me his grave on her family's land, buried in 1713. Nearby, I visited the site of a monastery founded by Saint Colmcille, the family's patron, circa 550 AD. Still standing is a well said to have magical curative powers.

I wrote the book to explore the lives of ordinary American women of the mid-1800s. In a time of few opportunities for their gender, these characters consistently found them. I also post on Bluesky under the title "The Storied Sisters Society." I explore current heroines of historical fiction, who also act courageously in pursuit of their dreams. These acts, real and imagined, were smaller than grand movements but, accumulated over time, are no less monumental.

MCGUIRK FAMILY TREE 1850

Torlough	Susan	Michael	Catherine	Francis H	Isabella	John L
McGuirk —	Fee	Heffernan —	McGuirk	McGuirk —	O'Brien	McGuirk
1821-1891	1828-1903	1824-1898	1824-1869	1825-1863	1826-1862	1829-1904

Francis H McGuirk	Mary E (Mamie) McGuirk
1848-1903	1848-1931

Notes

CHAPTER ONE

Missing Friends advertisement placed by Michael Heffernan in 1864
Ruth-Ann M. Harris, Donald M. Jacobs, and B. Emer O'Keeffe, eds., *Searching for Missing Friends: Irish Immigrant Advertisements Placed in the* Boston Pilot, vol. 5, *1861–1865* (Boston: New England Historic Genealogical Society, 1989), 365.

Murtagh MacEirc
Sidney Lee, ed., *Dictionary of National Biography*, vol. 39, *Morehead–Myles* (New York: Macmillan, 1894), 271.

Story of Termonmaguirk
Belmore, Somerset Richard Lowry-Corry, Earl of Belmore, *The History of the Two Ulster Manors of Finagh, in the County of Tyrone, and Coole, Otherwise Manor Atkinson, in the County of Fermanagh, and of Their Owners* (London: Longmans, Green & Company, 1881), 318.

Map of Termonmaguirk County Tyrone

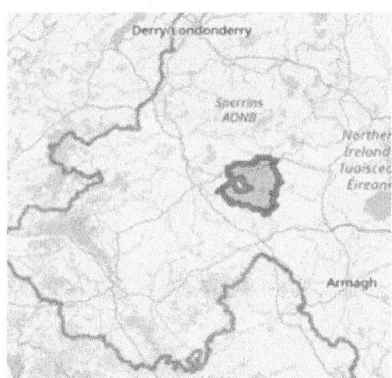

Map data © OpenStreetMap contributors

NOTES

Bell of Saint Colmcille

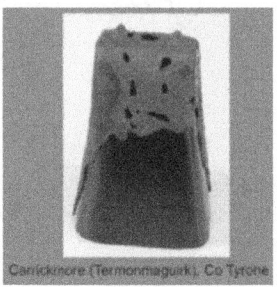

Bourke, Cormac. *The Early Medieval Hand-bells of Ireland and Britain.* (Ireland: Wordwell, *Published in association with the National Museum of Ireland*), pages 552, 553.

McGuirk's Farm in Ireland

The National Archives of Ireland, Tithe Applotment Books, 1823–1837, *Census of Mullinclavin, Magheracloone, Monaghan, Ireland, 1832.* Photograph by Susan McGuirk

Passage of Catherine and Terrence McGuirk and Patrick Lynch aboard the *Queen Victoria*

United States Bureau of Customs, *Passenger Lists of Vessels Arriving at New York, 1820–1897* (Washington: National Archives and Records Service, 1957), 180–89.

Erca, Princess of Dal Riata

Sidney Lee, ed., *Dictionary of National Biography*, vol. 39, *Morehead–Myles* (New York: Macmillan, 1894), 271.

NOTES

Main Street Village of Sag Harbor, New York

Photograph from the John Jermain Memorial Library Local History Archives Center

Cabra Castle, Kingscourt Ireland, Sir George Foster, owner 1840

Samuel Lewis, Topographical Dictionary of Ireland, *2nd ed., vol. 2 (London: S. Lewis & Co., 1837), 187. Creative Commons Attribution-Share Alike 2.0 Generic license. Photograph by Joseph Mischyshyn*

Shops on Main Street of Sag Harbor
Dorothy Zaykowski, *Sag Harbor: The Story of an American Beauty* (Sag Harbor: The Sag Harbor Historical Society, 1991), part III.

Nassau Hotel
Dorothy Zaykowski, *Sag Harbor: The Story of an American Beauty* (Sag Harbor: The Sag Harbor Historical Society, 1991), 199.

Herman Melville in Sag Harbor
Herman Melville, *Moby-Dick; or The Whale* (New York: Harper & Brothers, 1851), 67, 70, 282, 363.

Michael Heffernan's birth
Catholic Parish Registers at the NLI Cashel | Microfilm 02501 / 02 Diocese of Cashel and Emly | County of Tipperary
Baptisms 11 Nov. 1793 to 19 Jul. 1831 Page 145; Oct. 1826 to Nov. 1826.

NOTES

Irish Society School
Samuel Lewis, *Topographical Dictionary of Ireland*, 2nd ed., vol. 2 (London: S. Lewis & Co., 1837), 187.

Passage of Susan Fee
United States Bureau of Customs, *Passenger Lists of Vessels Arriving at New York, 1820–1897* (Washington: National Archives and Records Service, 1957), M237 Roll 57, 40.

Residence of William Heffernan in Southampton, New York
Kenneth Scott & Rosanne Conway, *New York Alien Residents, 1825–1848* (Baltimore: Genealogical Publishing Company, 1978), 51.

CHAPTER TWO

James Fenimore Cooper in Sag Harbor
James Fenimore Cooper, Correspondence of James Fenimore-Cooper, vol. 1 (New Haven: Yale University Press, 1922), 37.

Typical Whaling Route Between New York and the Sandwich Islands (Hawaii)

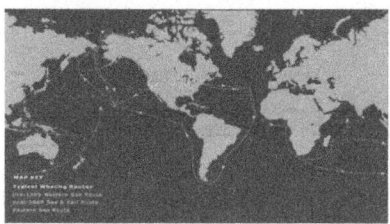

Courtesy of the Martha's Vineyard Museum

Record of Charles Fee as a whaler
William Donaldson Halsey, Sketches from Local History (Bridgehampton: H. Lee, 1935), 111.

Jane Perdue residence, 1850 US Census
United States Census 1850, East Hampton, NY, pg 348, dwelling #1219.

Mulford Family as Slaveholders
Allison Manfra McGovern, "Disrupting the Narrative: Labor and Survivance for the Montauketts of Eastern Long Island" (PhD diss., CUNY Graduate Center, 2015), 413
The National Archives in Washington, DC; Washington, DC; First Census of the United States, 1790.; Year: 1790; Census Place: East Hampton, Suffolk, New York; Series: M637; Roll: 6; Page: 150.

Whaling deity of Shinnecock and Montaukett tribes
"Whales and Subsistence Whalers," The Whaling Museum & Education Center, accessed May 21, 2024.

NOTES

Montaukett tribe scattered and Jane Perdue biographical note
Emily Button, "Navigating Difference: The Archaeology of Identities in an American Whaling Port" (PhD diss., Brown University, 2015), 330.

Saint David A.M.E. Zion Church, Sag Harbor, New York

Creative Commons Attribution-Share Alike 4.0 International license
Photograph by Capt JayRuffins

Marriage of Catherine McGuirk and Michael Heffernan
John H. Hunt, *The Fourth Book of Records of the Town of Southampton with a List of Soldiers and Sailors in the Union Forces of the Civil War* (Sag Harbor: John H. Hunt, 1896), 128.

CHAPTER THREE

Passage of Isabella O'Brien
United States Bureau of Customs, *Passenger Lists of Vessels Arriving at New York, 1820–1897* (Washington: National Archives and Records Service, 1957), M237 Roll 63, 402.

Wyandanch Hotel, Greenport, NY

George Bradford Brainerd Brooklyn Museum/Brooklyn Public Library, Brooklyn Collection

NOTES

Walt Whitman in Greenport
Walt Whitman, "Letters from Paumanok," in *The Walt Whitman* Archive, ed. Jason Stacy (27 June 1851). Gen. ed. Matt Cohen, Ed Folsom, and Kenneth M. Price.
Walt Whitman, *Notebooks and Unpublished Prose Manuscripts*, ed. Edward F. Grier (New York: New York University Press, 1984), 1:86–87.

Men of Sag Harbor leaving for the Gold Rush
Dorothy Zaykowski, *Sag Harbor: The Story of an American Beauty* (Sag Harbor: The Sag Harbor Historical Society, 1991), 106.

Silas Perdue's advertisement in the *Sag Harbor Corrector*
Letter stating that his wife Jane had left him after "robbing" him of bed and board, and that he would not pay any debts she accrued, *Sag Harbor Corrector*, December 6, 1848. Cited in Emily Button, *Navigating Difference: The Archaeology of Identities in an American Whaling Port* (PhD diss., Brown University, 2015), 311.

Book collection of Jane Perdue
Emily Button, "Navigating Difference: The Archaeology of Identities in an American Whaling Port" (PhD diss., Brown University, 2015), 180.

Birth of Mary Ellen "Mamie" McGuirk
Hunt, John H. *The Fourth Book of Records of the Town of Southampton with a list of Soldiers and Sailors in the Union Forces of the Civil War* (Sag Harbor, NY: John H. Hunt, 1896),149.

Possible record of Catherine Heffernan giving birth
John H. Hunt, *The Fourth Book of Records of the Town of Southampton with a List of Soldiers and Sailors in the Union Forces of the Civil War* (Sag Harbor: John H. Hunt, 1896), 156.

Jane Perdue's dreams
John Price, *Indians of Canada: Cultural Dynamic* (Scarborough, Ontario: Prentice-Hall of Canada, 1979), 81, 172.

Saint Andrew's Cemetery in Sag Harbor, New York

Courtesy of St. Andrew's Church, Sag Harbor, New York

NOTES

CHAPTER FOUR

Residence of Catherine and Ellen Heffernan, 1850 US Census
1850 New York Federal Population Census Schedules — New York City
United States Census 1850, New York, NY, Ward 5, p. 278, domicile #1019.
Provided in association with National Archives and Records Administration.

Map of 155 Hudson Street between Laight Street and Hubert Street New York City

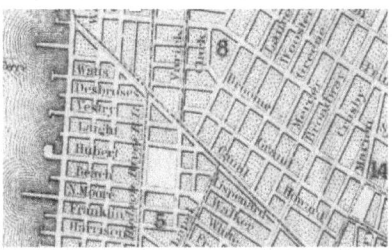

http://hdl.loc.gov/loc.gmd/g3804n.wd000512

Saint John's Park, Hudson Street, New York

(CC BY-SA 4.0GFDL)

Residences of Tor (translated) and Susan McGuirk, and Elisha Halsey 1850 US Census
United States Census 1850, Southampton, NY, pg 192, domicile # 74, domicile # 71.
Provided in association with the National Archives and Records Administration.

Residence of Frank and Isabella McGuirk, 1850 US Census
United States Census 1850, East Hampton, NY, pg 348, domicile # 1220.
Provided in association with the National Archives and Records Administration.

Residence of Patrick Lynch, 1850 US Census
United States Census 1850, New York City. New York, New York, Ward 3, p. 349, domicile #150, line 22.
Provided in association with the National Archives and Records Administration.

Passage of Patrick Lynch on business to Panama and Jamaica

NOTES

United States Bureau of Customs, *Passenger Lists of Vessels Arriving at New York, 1820–1897*, (Washington: National Archives and Records Service, 1957), M237 Roll 85, 561.

Passage of Patrick Lynch to San Francisco on business in 1850
Louis J. Rasmussen, *San Francisco Ship Passenger Lists*, vol. 1. 1850-1864 (Colma, California:
Louis J. Rasmussen, 1965); (Reprint: Baltimore: Genealogical Publishing Co., 1978).

Passage of Frank and Johnny McGuirk to the Gold Rush
Louis J. Rasmussen, *San Francisco Ship Passenger Lists*, vol. 2. [1850-1851] (Colma, California:
Clearfield Company Inc., 1966), 227.

Passage of Johnny McGuirk from Liverpool to New York
United States Bureau of Customs, "Passenger Lists of Vessels Arriving at New York, 1820–1897" (Washington: National Archives and Records Service, 1957) M237 Roll 89, 660.

CHAPTER FIVE

Saint Peter's Church, Barclay Street, New York City

Creative Commons Attribution-Share Alike 4.0 International, 3.0 Unported, 2.5 Generic, 2.0 Generic and 1.0 Generic license.
Photograph by Beyond My Ken

NOTES

Pierre Toussaint 1766–1853

By Anthony Meucci Gift of Georgina Schuyler Source: © Collection of the New-York Historical Society/Bridgeman Art Library

Grave of Pierre Toussaint at Old Saint Patrick's Cathedral Graveyard

263 Mulberry Street, New York City Creator: Manjari Sharma, photographer Source: © Curriculum Concepts International

Jane Perdue's collection
Emily Button, "Navigating Difference: The Archaeology of Identities in an American Whaling Port" (PhD diss., Brown University, 2015), 183.

Women's Rights Convention
Document 15: Proceedings of the Woman's Rights Convention, held at the Broadway Tabernacle, in the City of New York, on Tuesday and Wednesday, Sept. 6th and 7th, 1853 (New York: Fowler and Wells, Publishers, 1853), 96.

Passage of Frank and Johnny McGuirk from the Gold Rush to New York
United States Bureau of Customs, *Passenger Lists of Vessels Arriving at New York, 1820–1897* (Washington: National Archives and Records Service, 1957), M237 Roll 150, 434, 436.

Advertisement placed by Walt Whitman for *Leaves of Grass*
Blalock, Stephanie. "Documents Related to the 1855 Leaves of Grass: Early Draft

NOTES

Advertisements." The Walt Whitman Archive. Gen. ed. Matt Cohen, Ed Folsom, & Kenneth M. Price. Accessed 24 July 2025.

Passage of Patrick Lynch to Nicaragua
United States Bureau of Customs, *Passenger Lists of Vessels Arriving at New York, 1820-1897* (Washington: National Archives and Records Service, 1957), M237 Roll 158, 166, 58unix/page/n165/.

Passage of Michael Heffernan from the Gold Rush to New York
United States Bureau of Customs, *Passenger Lists of Vessels Arriving at New York, 1820-1897* (Washington: National Archives and Records Service, 1957), M237 Roll 150, 78.

Whaling Log of the *Bark Neva* recorded by Michael Heffernan

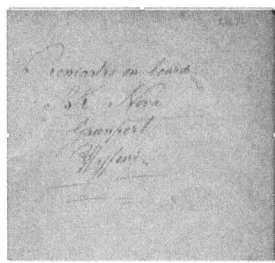

George A. Conklin, Journal kept by George A. Conklin on board bark Neva from Greenport, George L. Hand, master, bound for Pacific, Sep 28, 1857–Oct 20, 1859. Courtesy of the East Hampton Library, Long Island Collection

St. Colmcille's exile on the island of Iona
Thomas Cahill, *How the Irish Saved Civilization: The Untold Story of Ireland's Heroic Role from the Fall of Rome to the Rise of Medieval Europe* (New York: Doubleday, 1995), 171.

Residence of Betsey Fee Josey and John "Joe" Josey, 1860 US Census
1860 United States Federal Census, Southampton, NY, p. 14, dwelling #101. Provided in association with the National Archives and Records Administration.

John "Joe" Josey voyage
Bark Byron: 1855-1857
American Offshore Whaling Database
Creative Commons Attribution 4.0 International License
New Bedford Whaling Museum

CHAPTER SIX

Residence of Joseph Bose in Canada
1851 Census of Canada East, p. 31.
Public Archives of Canada Microfilmed 1955.

NOTES

Residence of Tor (translated) and Susan McGuirk 1860 US Census
1860 United States Federal Census, Southampton, NY, p. 14, dwelling #844.
Provided in association with the National Archives and Records Administration.

Tomasina Farm Bridgehampton, New York

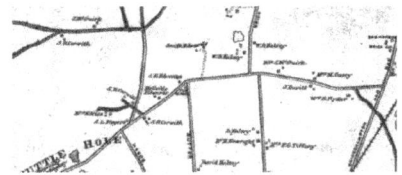

1900 Map of Bridgehampton Compiled by William Halsey, drawn by Godfrey H. Baldwin, 1924. William Donaldson Halsey,
Sketches from Local History *(Bridgehampton: H. Lee, 1935), 204.*

Residence of Johnny McGuirk and niece Mary E. "Mamie" McGuirk 1860 US Census
1860 United States Federal Census, Southampton, NY, p. 68, dwelling #1264, #1263.
Provided in association with the National Archives and Records Administration.

Residence of Catherine Heffernan, Patrick Lynch, and Bose family 1860 US Census
1860 United States Federal Census, New York City Ward 1, p. 80, dwelling #152.
Provided in association with the National Archives and Records Administration.

Death of Michael "Mickey" Lynch
New York City Municipal Archives; New York, NY, USA; Manhattan Vital Registers; Source Record Group: RG 095 Vital Records.

Residence of Frank McGuirk, 1860 US Census
1860 United States Federal Census, Southampton, NY, p. 44, dwelling #1085.
Provided in association with the National Archives and Records Administration.

Residence of Isabella McGuirk, 1860 US Census
1860 United States Federal Census, Southampton, NY, p. 70, dwelling #1279.
Provided in association with the National Archives and Records Administration.

Residence of Jane Perdue, 1860 US Census
1860 United States Federal Census, Easthampton, NY, p. 508, dwelling #358.
Provided in association with the National Archives and Records Administration.

Patrick Lynch's war service
Vol 11 - 85 N.Y. S. V.
Muster In Roll of the First Regiment of US Chasseurs Volunteers, Company C July 11, 1861
p. 679 (7). DMNA NY
Yale University Archive

NOTES

CHAPTER SEVEN

Record of Frank and Johnny McGuirk volunteering for the Civil War
William Donaldson Halsey, *Sketches from Local History* (Bridgehampton: H. Lee, 1935), 85.

Frank McGuirk's war service
New York State Military Museum and Veterans Research Center 165th Infantry Regiment
Nickname: Second Battalion Duryea's Zouaves; Smith's Zouaves. REPORT OF THE ADJUTANT-GENERAL.
McGUIRK, FRANK.— Age, 36 years. Enlisted, September 10, 1862, at New York City, to serve three years; mustered in as private, Co. C, November 28, 1862; killed in action, May 27, 1863, before Port Hudson, La.

Record of George Perdue as a whaleman
Bark Joshua Braydon: 1853-1857
American Crew List Database
Creative Commons Attribution 4.0 International License
New Bedford Whaling Museum

U.S., Civil War Draft Registrations Records, 1863-1865 for George Perdue
The National Archives in Washington, DC; Washington, DC, USA; *Consolidated Lists of Civil War Draft Registration Records (Provost Marshal General's Bureau; Consolidated Enrollment Lists, 1863-1865)*; Record Group: *110*; Collection Name: *Consolidated Enrollment Lists, 1863-1865 (Civil War Union Draft Records)*; NAI: *4213514*; Archive Volume Number: *2 of 3*

Johnny McGuirk's second enlistment in the Civil War
James Truslow Adams, *History of the Town of Southampton (East of Canoe Place)* (Bridgehampton: Hampton Press, 1918), "List of Soldiers and Sailors in Civil War," 398.

Missing Friends advertisement placed by Ellen Heffernan in 1864
Ruth-Ann M. Harris, Donald M. Jacobs, and B. Emer O'Keeffe, eds., *Searching for Missing Friends: Irish Immigrant Advertisements Placed in the* Boston Pilot, vol. 5, *1861–1865* (Boston: New England Historic Genealogical Society, 1989), 258.

NOTES

CHAPTER EIGHT

Marriage Bans of Delphina Bechet in Paris, France

Archives de Paris et sa région: Publications des bans de Mariages 1860-1930. *Paris: ARFIDO S.A., 2006. © ARFIDO S.A.*

Death of Patrick Lynch
Date of Interment: November, 28 1868
System: CEM
Section: LETT | Row: A | Plot: 53
Holy Cross Cemetery, Brooklyn, New York.

Doctor John "Jack" McGuirk residence
H. Wilson, *Trow's New York City Directory*, vol. 83, for the Year ending May 1, 1870 (New York: John F. Trow, 1870), 739, source 707.

Missing Friends advertisement placed by Michael Heffernan in 1868
Ruth-Ann M. Harris, Donald M. Jacobs, and B. Emer O'Keeffe, eds., *Searching for Missing Friends: Irish Immigrant Advertisements Placed in the* Boston Pilot, vol. 6, *1866–1870* (Boston: New England Historic Genealogical Society, 1989), 396.

NOTES

Record of Michael Heffernan's bequest to wife, Catherine, from *Sag Harbor Corrector* 1868

BRIDGHAMPTON.

The Heffernan place, at the "Old Farm," was finally bought by Mrs. Mary Casey, wife of John Casey, for the sum of $2,200.

Samuel H. Howell has sold a lot of about 10 acres of land, in Mecox, near Swan Creek, to Michael Howard, for $700.

Hiram S. Rogers has bought about 10 acres of land near the Bridgehampton Railroad depot, of the estate of Wm. Fordham, dec'd for $825.

Edward Howell of Poxabogue, is

Portrait of Elizabeth Seton by an unknown artist

Collection of St. Peter's Church, Barclay Street, New York, NY

NOTES

CHAPTER NINE

Grave of Silas and Jane Perdue in Saint David A.M.E. Zion Church Graveyard

Photograph by Susan McGuirk

Death record of Catherine Heffernan
Holy Cross Cemetery, Brooklyn, NY.
U.S. Census Mortality Schedules, New York, 1850-1880; New York State Education Department, Office of Cultural Education; *Albany, New York*; Year: *1870*; Roll: *M7*; Line Number: *26*
Provided in association with the National Archives and Records Administration.

Civil War service record of Michael Heffernan
Official Roster of the Soldiers of the State of Ohio in the War of the Rebellion, 1861–1866, vol. 5 (Akron: Werner, 1887), 310.

Maritime Underground Railroad
Southampton Press, August 27, 2014. Historical Society Sets Out To Uncover Sag Harbor's Involvement With The Underground Railroad.
Walker, Timothy D., editor. *Sailing to Freedom: Maritime Dimensions of the Underground Railroad*. University of Massachusetts Press, 2021.

EPILOGUE
Employment of Francis McGuirk in Brooklyn
Brooklyn City and Business Directory for the year ending May 1, 1869.

Banking Records of Catherine Heffernan
Emigrant Savings Bank. *Emigrant Savings Bank Records*. Call number *R-USLHG *ZI-815. Rolls 1-20. New York Public Library, New York, New York.

Residence of John Josey, 1870 US Census
Population schedules of the ninth census of the United States, 1870, New York, p. 336, dwelling #283.

NOTES

Provided in association with the National Archives and Records Administration.

Cross Street in Sag Harbor. Photograph by Susan McGuirk

Residence of Jane Perdue, 1870 US Census
Population schedules of the ninth census of the United States, 1870, New York, p. 40, dwelling #310, #7. Provided in association with the National Archives and Records Administration. Emily Button, "Navigating Difference: The Archaeology of Identities in an American Whaling Port" (PhD diss., Brown University, 2015), 138.

Liberty Street in Sag Harbor. Photograph by Susan McGuirk

Residence of Johnny McGuirk, 1870 US Census
Population schedules of the ninth census of the United States, 1870, New York, p. 374, dwelling #594.
Provided in association with the National Archives and Records Administration.

Residence of Michael Heffernan, 1870 US Census
Population schedules of the ninth census of the United States, 1870, Ohio, p. 254, dwelling #256.
Provided in association with the National Archives and Records Administration.

Residence of Tor (translated) McGuirk and Doctor John "Jack" McGuirk, 1870 Census
Population schedules of the ninth census of the United States, 1870, New York, p. 368, dwelling #538.
Provided in association with the National Archives and Records Administration.

Acknowledgments

Many thanks go to my publisher, Mary Petiet, for all her help and belief in me. For all their encouragement along the way, I thank Leslie Budnick, Susan Chang, Jacquelin Cangro, Eliza Dee and Lila LaBine.

The late, great Dorothy Zaykowski deserves much thanks for her interest and advice when I met her years ago at the Sag Harbor Historical Society. I want to thank Sandi Brewster-walker, the Executive Director of the Montaukett Indian Nation, for her invaluable help, advice, and encouragement. Sarah Clark, an Algonquin expert, deserves much appreciation for her thoughtful insight and wisdom.

Many thanks to the Sag Harbor Whaling & Historical Museum, the staffs of the East Hampton Library, Rogers Memorial Library in Southampton, the Suffolk County Historical Society in Riverhead, the John Jermain Memorial Library in Sag Harbor, the Westhampton Free Library, the Milstein Division of U.S., Local History and Genealogy at the New York Public Library, the New York Society Library, and the Nantucket Whaling Museum.

My deep thanks and appreciation go to Larry McDermott, the local historian in Carrickmacross, Ireland. Also, deep thanks go to Nuala McGurk and her family of Carrickmore, Northern Ireland.

I am most indebted to the authors of two dissertations that deeply informed my research: Emily Button and Allison Manfra McGovern. Another author who deserves many thanks is the late John L. Strong for his life's dedication to the Native Americans of Eastern Long Island.

Finally, I would like to thank my book cover designer, Kathleen Lynch, for her artistry and expertise.

Book Club Guide

The following is food for thought for book club members to consider and share. Some readers may prefer concentrating on issues of character and personality. Others may choose to emphasize themes and meanings in their discussions. Either approach may lead to lively and fruitful exchanges.

• Is there a character you would befriend and why?

• Did letter writing play a comparable role in the book to emails and texts today?

• What role did books play in the character's lives? Who were affected by them and in what way?

• Did the characters have expectations for their lives that were in line with their circumstances? Did they expect too much or settle for too little?

• Sisterhood is a theme in the book even though most of the women characters do not have sisters. Can the experience be duplicated in a friendship or as an in-law through marriage?

• How did needing, seeking, and finding employment steer individual lives in the book?

• Losing family members of all ages was common in the mid-1800s. Did the characters move past loss differently than we do today?

- When did Cath ask for permission and when did she not?

- Did Cath have regrets? If given the chance to start over, would she have made different choices?

- What might Cath have done had she lived past the age of 46?

About the Author

Courtesy Billy Farrell/BFA.com

Susan McGuirk posts about historical fiction heroines on her blog "The Storied Sisters Society" on Bluesky and on her website, www.susanmcguirk.com. Susan worked at Anthology Film Archives, a historical film museum and honed her writing skills at HBO programming, composing hundreds of in-house film reviews. She earned a BA and MA in Media Studies from the New School and lives with her husband in New York City. To learn more about Susan, scan below.

About The Press

Sea Crow Press

Sea Crow Press publishes compelling fiction, nonfiction, and poetry with strong voice, deep heart, and a connection to the natural world. From the windswept shores of Cape Cod to imagined climate futures, our books inspire, engage, and endure.

We are committed to amplifying voices and sharing stories that matter. Alongside our acclaimed eco-lit and regional titles, we publish historical fiction and immigrant stories that illuminate the resilience of individuals and communities across time and place. These narratives deepen our mission by honoring cultural memory, celebrating diverse experiences, and revealing the ways in which history and migration shape both people and landscapes.

At Sea Crow Press, every book reflects our belief that stories rooted in place can move the world. To learn more about Sea Crow Press, scan below.